BBC NATIONAL SHORT STORY AWARD 2023

BBC National Short Story Award 2023

with Cambridge University

First published in Great Britain in 2023 by Comma Press.
www.commapress.co.uk

Copyright © remains with the authors 2023.
This collection copyright © Comma Press 2023.

'Churail' by Kamila Shamsie first published in *Furies* (Virago, March, 2023). 'It's Me' by K Patrick first published in *Five Dials* (Hamish Hamilton, Spring, 2023).

The moral rights of the contributors to be identified as the authors of this work have been asserted in accordance with the Copyright Designs and Patents Act 1988. All rights reserved. No part of this publication may be reproduced, stored in a retrieval system or transmitted in any form, or by any means (electronic, mechanical, or otherwise), without the written permission of both the copyright holders and the publisher.

A CIP catalogue record of this book is available from the British Library.

ISBN-10: 1-912697-74-2
ISBN-13: 978-1-91269-774-8

The publisher gratefully acknowledges the support of Arts Council England.

Printed and bound in Great Britain by Clays Ltd, Elcograf S.p.A

Contents

INTRODUCTION Reeta Chakrabarti	VII
CHURAIL Kamila Shamsie	1
THE STORM Nick Mulgrew	15
COMORBIDITIES Naomi Wood	39
GUESTS Cherise Saywell	61
IT'S ME K Patrick	79
ABOUT THE AUTHORS	99
ABOUT THE AWARD	103
AWARD PARTNERS	107

Introduction

ANYONE PICKING UP THIS volume has a treat in store, because here are five of the best in English modern short story writing. The five of us on the judging panel read dozens of entries, providing – for me at least – a crash course in contemporary short-form fiction. I've learnt many things from being a judge on this wonderful prize, and key among them is that the short story leaves the author absolutely nowhere to hide. It's a tight, structured format which demands discipline and precision; the writer has none of the novelist's luxury of digression or padding. The five stories we have chosen were the most glittering - five jewels of succinct, beautifully-calibrated writing.

As a broadcast journalist, storytelling is my day job. I have spent my career crafting and shaping words, principally of course to impart information. But as well as explaining complicated politics or policies, journalism is also about conveying the

INTRODUCTION

emotion of the people we film and interview. They may have been through bereavement or tragedy, be suffering homelessness or financial loss. Abroad, they may be civilians in a country at war, or displaced people fleeing conflict or poverty or both. They may fear their forests burning or their villages flooding. Young people faced with limited choices may fear for their future. A typical television news report is only two and a half minutes long – even a 'special' report is rarely more than five minutes. It's a short story boiled down to its most condensed form.

That's as far as the analogy goes, because of course we deal in fact not fiction, and have none of these authors' aesthetic tools at our disposal – of imagination and the creative refashioning of the world, the use of myth, the metaphysical, or satire. But I was struck by how much the themes in this year's competition were common to those we are absorbed by in news. The judges read repeatedly of fears of climate change, of harsh environments and of general eco-anxieties; and also of youthful anxiety, stories of young people trying to navigate an impersonal world and feeling disconnected from it. Other themes that kept recurring included displacement: young adults in a foreign country which they cannot read and where they don't know how to behave. Several stories had an element of fantasy and the

INTRODUCTION

supernatural; those that worked best read like fables, the paranormal underlining a point more effectively than a realistic tale.

My fellow judges – Jessie Burton, Roddy Doyle, Okechukwu Nzelu and Di Speirs – and I had a challenging task. We did not know each other, although Jessie and I had sat on a panel together before. Neither did we know the identities of the authors, so could not be swayed by a big name, and those who appear here are on merit alone. It was a hard choice, and we all had to let go of some stories that we had championed, but we all agreed that these five were the best of their kind.

'The Storm' by Nick Mulgrew is a simple story worked to perfection. Daringly it has, at its heart, a repulsive and aggressive character, a father who takes out his resentment against his ex-wife by using her swimming pool when she is not there, while being watched by his nervous, timorous son. The backdrop is a brewing storm, with the whole short scene told from the point of view of the boy's young friend. The judges thought this was a brilliant, well-written story, and one in which we all responded viscerally to the father. The portrayal moved one judge to say emphatically, 'I was so disappointed that the father didn't...' well I won't spoil the ending for you. We felt the story described real jeopardy, and the relationship between the two boys was well worked and original. The son wrestles with his fear of, but also his love for, his father, lending this piece a deep poignancy that stayed with us.

K Patrick's 'It's Me' is a different genre entirely, a story of a chance meeting in a café between two young people after several years, with the author playing with our notions of identity and gender. The judges felt the author was brave to portray this period of early 20s life without feeling that everything needs explanation or resolution. The piece is full of literary references which were judged to be on the right side of cleverness, and the structure impels the reader towards an ending that is also a beginning. There is a striking sparsity to the language, and some of the imagery is startling: 'handfuls of rocket like cut hair' and 'car tyres blurting through puddles.' In a year in which many of the stories were about attraction and sexual desire, this one stood out.

'Guests' by Cherise Saywell is a many-layered and devastatingly effective tale. Two women, one a refugee with a small boy, the other a Westerner, live side by side in an unnamed third country, next to a house with (again) a swimming pool. Natalie, who is 'five years out of school' when she arrives, and has 'gone nowhere, done nothing,' likes to float in the pool and smoke marijuana with her boyfriend Kurt when the owner is away, crawling through a crack in the fence that divides them. Bilen's little boy is fascinated by the pool. What ensues was judged by the panel to be a brilliant inversion of the refugee crisis discourse, one that was clever and full of dignity. The action takes place around a ritual of coffee-grinding and coffee-making, which was precise and elegant and loaded with meaning. The author very cleverly balances opposing themes of dispossession and entitlement, purpose and shiftlessness. A really first-rate piece of writing!

'Churail' by Kamila Shamsie is similarly a stunning piece of work, with what one judge called 'a banger of an opening paragraph!' A father leaves Pakistan with his young daughter after his wife passes away, fleeing the myth of the churail, by which women who die in childbirth 'call out to their victims in the sweetest of voices,' luring men to their hiding place and keeping them there, 'draining them of their life force.' This story is a deft and witty exploration of myth and superstition and the misogyny underpinning them; of remaking yourself as an immigrant and the limits of doing so; all delivered with a great metaphysical twist at the end. The piece is beautifully written and, at under three thousand words, done with great economy. There are no wrong tones or false registers, it is deeply impressive.

INTRODUCTION

Last but not least (her surname starts with W) Naomi Wood's 'Comorbidities' was one of the few genuinely funny stories among this year's entries, written with a light and wry touch, but also tackling some serious themes. At its centre is an exhausted young mother who adores her children, and who is consumed by anxiety for the state of the planet. Her subtle mother-in-law, who wants a third grandchild, offers to have the children for a day to give the couple some romantic time together, time which they use to make a video of themselves. The judges thought this was an elegant and topical story, which cleverly combines contemporary fears about climate change and the internet, with great comic timing. The open ending leaves the reader guessing – is this about averting the disasters you can, and valuing what you have?

I do hope I have whetted your appetite for the stories to come. If you enjoy them half as much as we all did, you will be in for a feast.

Reeta Chakrabarti
London, 2023

Churail

Kamila Shamsie

My father migrated to England with me weeks after I was born to protect us from my mother, who had died giving birth to me. My cousin, Zainab, informed me of my starring role in this turn of events when I was six years old and my father was preparing to move us to London from Manchester, where we'd been living with Zainab's parents. It's important to hear the truth, Zainab told me, with the solemnity of an eleven-year-old who doesn't know when she might ever again see her young cousin. There were four miscarriages before I came along, and after the second the doctors advised against further pregnancies. My mother talked of adoption, but my father was insistent that he must have a son of his own blood, and the universe responded as it does when men refuse to understand what nature is trying to tell them: it gave him the wrong kind of child, and it took away his wife.

It was summer. We were sitting on the floor of Zainab's bedroom, which she'd consented to share with me since I was old enough to be moved out of the crib next to my aunt's bedside. Serena Williams and One Direction looked down at us as the July rain blurred the world outside in its predictable way. Zainab took my hand in hers. The next bit was the most important, she said.

I was only days old when my father heard a woman's voice calling his name from the peepul tree that grew across the street from our home. He looked up at the first call, strode to the door at the second, and was bloodless with terror, immobilised, when no third call came. My wet-nurse saw it all, and she was the one to spread it through our village that my mother had become a churail.

Women who died in childbirth often became churail, and were known for their fondness for living in peepul trees and calling out to their victims in the sweetest of voices. A misty dark night was the most dangerous time to be enticed by a churail because you might see only the beauty of her face and miss the telltale sign of feet turned backwards at the ankle. The other clue to the churail was that she would always call her victim's name twice – never once, never three times. She would lure men to her hiding place and keep them there, draining them of their life force, until they were old and spent. When she released them back into the world they'd find decades had gone by and everyone they knew was dead, so they would end their lives alone and unloved.

'Basically, Rip van Winkle is the story of a man spirited away by a churail but with the sex censored,' Zainab said, briefly her usual self, trying to throw the word 'sex' in my direction at any opportunity just to see me squirm. Then she turned serious again: 'When your father says he'll never go back to Pakistan because it's a terrible place, don't believe him. He won't go back because he's afraid the churail is waiting for him.'

We moved from Manchester to London when I was six, from Wembley to Queen's Park when I was eight, and from Queen's Park to Kensington when I was nine. With the move from one Kensington property to the next, my father's life finally caught up with his ambitions when I was twelve. He bought a house with a garden – the seventh largest in London, six places down from Buckingham Palace – and said we would never move again. You can make friends now, he said, as though it were the change in addresses rather than the awkwardness and insecurity of my character that had impeded my social life. He sent me to the most expensive school he could find and told me not to mix with the wrong kind of girl, by which I knew he meant other Pakistanis. He had huge disdain for his brother who had moved to England without any interest in becoming English: 'If you enter someone's home as a guest you must find ways of being pleasing to them,' he liked to say. His way of being pleasing to the English was to take up squash, hire an accent coach, become a donor to the arts and a member of a venerable men-only club. But his attempts to showcase me as the perfect immigrant daughter resulted in disappointment: the piano teacher, the tennis coach, the French au pairs left only the faintest impression, quickly smudged.

One day he came home to find me in the kitchen, and, although I wasn't doing anything other than bending down to the vegetable drawer in our fridge on my way to assembling a sandwich, the sight of me made him cry out in rage.

'No matter what I do you'll always look like a peasant working in the fields,' he said.

And then a miracle occurred. When I was sixteen, Zainab moved to London for an investment banking job after a glittering turn at university. She was everything my father wanted me to be: stylish, skilled in small-talk, ambitious, opening bat for the City Ladies Cricket Club. He

CHURAIL

encouraged her to treat our home as though it were hers, seemed pleased whenever he saw her walk through the front door, laughed at her jokes, asked about her life. I couldn't hate her for it, and she quickly took up her old position as the shining centre of my life. In return, she appeared to find genuine pleasure in my company, which made me relax and talk openly with her in a way I never did with anyone else.

Her reappearance brought back an old memory, and one afternoon I asked her about the churail.

She typed something into her phone as we reclined on adjoining garden chairs under the umbrella on an unnaturally hot autumn day.

'Listen! These are all the circumstances under which a woman can become a churail...'

Dying in childbirth, that was the first. Also, dying during pregnancy.

Dying during the period of lying-in (we had to look up 'lying-in', which didn't mean a lazy Sunday morning). Dying in bed.

Dying while on your period. Dying in any unnatural or tragic way. Dying after a life during which the woman has experienced abuse at the hands of a man. Dying after a life during which the woman has experienced abuse at the hands of her in-laws. Dying after a life of little or no sexual fulfilment.

'Well!' Zainab said.

Soon we were shouting out names of dead women who were clearly now churail: Marilyn Monroe (died in bed); Zainab's one-time neighbour Aunty Rubina (no sexual fulfilment, obviously); Amy Winehouse (unnatural death); Carrie Fisher (tragic death, because no matter how Princess Leia dies it's tragic); Princess Diana (in-laws).

Later that day, my father asked what Zainab and I had been laughing about so hysterically he had to close the windows to his study. He was on his way out when he asked this, front-door keys in his hand, and I knew the remark was a rebuke phrased as a question but even so I chose to answer it:

'Churail.'

He slipped the keys into his pocket, but not before I heard them jangle in his usually steady hand.

'Superstitious nonsense,' he said, and departed, leaving me alone. We had dispensed with au pairs when I turned thirteen, and instead he had cameras all over the house, presumably so he could replay the footage of any disaster that might kill or maim or assault me while he was out. This was the sort of thing I thought often and never said out loud, except to Zainab.

The next day Zainab texted to say my father had banned her from seeing me any more. When I went weeping to my father, he said, 'Exactly the kind of bad influence I've tried my whole life to keep you away from.'

A tiny part of me was relieved that I wouldn't have to watch him around Zainab and know he wasn't incapable of love, just that he was incapable of loving me.

My father's version of our migration story was this: when my mother died, my uncle called from Manchester and said his business was expanding, he could do with my father's help and my aunt would raise me with Zainab as my older sister. And so my father came to England, mostly for my sake. It was only once he'd arrived that he saw two things: (a) the country he had left was a dump to which he intended never to return, and (b) he could become a rich man here, but not while attached to his brother's mini-cab company. There were several failed ventures before he made his first million from a marriage app targeting a Muslim clientele ('Discounts on venue hire, catering, car service and outfit tailoring for all our satisfied customers!').

'Why didn't you ever marry again?' I asked when I could speak to him once more. 'Didn't you want a son?' Sometimes there were short-term girlfriends in his life, but I was certain that most of his relations with women were uncomplicatedly transactional.

'Not once I understood there are other ways to leave a legacy,' he said. He was a man who liked to stamp his name on things – university scholarships, renovated theatre foyers, museum wings.

'And what am I?' I said.

He switched on the TV and turned his attention to *Dancing with the Stars*.

I continued to see Zainab, but furtively. She didn't set foot in our house again until the following summer when she entered no further than the hallway, front door open behind her, and asked me to let my father know she would like to talk to him.

It was the summer of floods in Pakistan, devastation without precedent. Zainab had quit her investment banking job, and was on her way to Pakistan to help with flood relief. She told my father she had come to see him, hat in hand (she was wearing a fedora, which she doffed in his direction as she spoke), to ask for a donation to the aid organisation she would be working with. His village was underwater, she said.

'My village is Kensington and Chelsea,' he said, and turned on his heels, still nimble in his movements despite his increased girth.

'Your family has lost everything,' she called out. 'Your uncles, your cousins.'

He didn't falter as he continued down the hall to his study, and I remembered the only time I had seen his body betray the tiniest disruption to his psyche.

I walked Zainab down the street to the nearest cash machine so I could withdraw the maximum amount my debit card allowed, and our conversation returned to the churail, who had led first to my exile from Pakistan, then Zainab's expulsion from my home.

'She's the victim of patriarchy who enacts revenge on men,' I said. 'I guess that's kind of feminist?'

'Except she's evil,' Zainab said. 'And she's evil because she's attractive and without sexual restraint.'

'She's a manifestation of patriarchy's guilt,' I said.

'She allows guilty men to cast themselves as

the victims,' Zainab said.

'And even when they're the victims they make themselves sex-gods with a fifty-year-long erection that a woman of unearthly beauty can't get enough of.'

Zainab laughed and laughed.

'Be this version of yourself more,' she said.

'Seriously, there are no queer churail?'

'Yes, like that, like that.'

I told Zainab that when I turned eighteen I would go to our family's village and visit my mother's grave. But when she returned from Pakistan it was with the news that the graveyard had been washed away in the flooding, along with every home in the village. Even the peepul tree, she said, even that had been destroyed. She placed a green-brown section of branch in my hand, six or seven inches long, with small heart-shaped leaves growing from it. 'This was the only thing I could bring back for you,' she said. 'Think of it as a climate refugee.'

'A climate refugee in a hostile environment,' I said, knowing that peepul trees can't grow in England. They want sun and humidity to thrive. Even so, I planted the cutting in the corner of our garden where there was the most sunlight. It was still summer in England, and hotter than any summer before. In the next weeks it grew a few centimetres, and then autumn came, and winter after, and though the peepul tree didn't die it stagnated, a stubby sad thing that the gardener wanted to uproot until our cook from Sri Lanka told him it had religious significance. My father was unaware of this piece of his village growing in the English garden he treated as entirely ornamental for visitors to look at admiringly from the windows of the house.

The following year, the summer heat came earlier, more ferociously. By June we already had hosepipe bans in London and the grass in the garden was burnt, the trees wilted. One weekend morning only a trickle of water came from the kitchen tap. We thought at first it was the drought, but every other tap gushed water. My father said he would call a plumber and I thought no more of it until I heard my father roaring my name from a corner of the garden I hadn't walked to in months.

The peepul was five or so feet high, its heart-shaped leaves thick and glossy. The plumber had his phone in his hand, one of those apps open that identifies plants. He called it 'invasive'; he said it could send its roots deep and far in search of water. It had entered our pipes, might already be burrowing its way into the foundation of the house.

'How is this here?' my father said.

I told him Zainab had brought it, clipped from the peepul tree across the street from the house in which I was born.

His face! Like a man receiving news of a sickness so old and deep in him that there's no way of cutting it out without excising his organs with it.

The plumber, reading off the screen, said we would have to call in an expert to remove it. Cut down the plant and the roots would continue to grow. Hard to know what damage had already been done.

That night my father stood in the rarely used drawing room, looking out at the seventh largest garden in London. We'd been leaving the windows open at night to let in the breeze but as I walked through the house in search of him I saw that each one was closed and locked. I went to stand beside him.

'Do you see her?' he said.

It was a spindly little thing, with nothing of the magnificence of the broad-trunked peepul I'd seen in pictures, with their aerial roots, their great height. We stood there a long time, the only sound his breath, strange and ragged. He didn't seem aware of my presence, appeared not to notice that I hadn't answered his question. The moon slid out from cloud; the breeze stirred the branches and leaves. I saw a slender-limbed figure hold out her arms towards the house. I heard a voice say a name, twice.

My name.

My father looked at me.

Very calmly, as if I had been waiting for this all my life, I walked towards the French windows and unbolted them. My father's hand clamped onto my wrist.

'She won't like it if you do that,' I said, and he moved his hand away as though my skin were poison.

I stepped into the garden. Dead grass beneath my bare feet. Across the burnt expanse the tree waited. Perhaps I would find my cousin Zainab hiding in the darkness. Perhaps I would find the real truth of the churail, a creature much older than the myths men wove around her, desperate to be the centre of her story.

One step and then another and another. I stopped, sat on the grass, and hugged my legs to my chest, my face turned up to the sky. There was no rush. I would sit there awhile, and my father would stand and watch me while the echo of the churail's voice burrowed deep inside him, shaking every foundation.

The Storm

Nick Mulgrew

THE FIRST DISTANT RUMBLE sounded. The man in the pool didn't react. Neither did Clement. Instead Clement watched his friend Dirk's dad stand, waist-deep and dripping, a can of beer in one hand, a cigarette in the other. The water was clean and clear, except for all the leaves at the bottom. A few remained floating on the surface, borne somehow, as if magnetically, toward Mr Wilson.

'Dad?'

'Yes, Dirkie.'

'Are– are you–?' While Dirk stuttered, his father took a drag from his fresh-lit Gunston, and after pausing a moment for a glug of beer, cast his gaze upward and exhaled. The smoke streamed from inside him, blending into the slowly deepening grey above them. The performance over, Dirk tried again. 'Are you sure you should be smoking?'

'I always smoke.' The man took another drag, deeper this time. He sighed strands of white as an urgent rustle sounded deep in the garden, if you could call it that. The three of them turned and stared into the expanse. Apart from where it had been cleared for the front gate, the jungle entirely surrounded Dirk's house, a boundary more imposing than the vibracrete wall that fronted onto the street. The innumerable arms of palm trees and evergreens formed an errant canopy, erasing all traces of the suburb beyond, save for one opening that framed a tall deciduous tree in someone's garden across the road, luxuriant in its isolation. From somewhere else came the intermittent tick of a broken electric fence – but no more movement. It must have been a bird.

'Your mother's boyfriend should get a gardener,' Dirk's dad said, finally. He raised the can of beer to his mouth.

Dirk ignored him. 'I know you smoke, Dad. I mean, just – are you sure you should be smoking *now*?'

'I'm training my lungs.'

'I *know*, it's just–'

'If you *knew*,' Dirk's dad snapped, 'then you wouldn't bloody *ask*.' The pool water gurgled as he turned toward the two boys. He brought the cigarette to his mouth, and his eyes widening at them, sucked on it angrily, until the roach glowed like a coal. He extinguished the remaining nub of the cigarette on the water's surface; it hissed in unison with his out-breath. He then flicked the filter into the beige and green thatch of buffalo lawn, into which it was instantly subsumed. 'I'm going for my best today,' he said, before draining the last of his beer, and wading over to the pool's edge to place it on the chipped slasto, near the boys' feet. He then returned to where he was, standing, waist-deep, in the middle of the pool. He began to suck in air, then expel it out his open mouth, tensing his belly until the tops of his abs threatened to show through. After ten or so rounds of breath, Dirk's dad pressed a little button on the side of his wristwatch, and with an attendant beep, submerged himself. Under the water, the man crouched to the bottom of the pool, where he sat, cross-legged, completely motionless. Dirk picked up the empty can, and went back to the house.

Clement, too, stayed still. He had said very little since he'd arrived at Dirk's. He hadn't even been there ten minutes when Dirk's father rattled the gates open and shuddered his yellow Cortina up the drive, Radio 5 sounding from the open windows. Clement had not been expecting parental supervision. Dirk's mom Sandy was away as she normally was, doing something, somewhere. Usually she'd come home later than the boys could force themselves to stay up. That's why Dirk's dad was here: because she wasn't. While Dirk had gone to close the gate, his dad exited the car with his duffel bag already in hand, said 'howzit' to Clement, and walked barefoot to the covered front veranda. There, under the rust-tinged metal awning, he'd immediately begun to strip, folding his T-shirt onto the back of the same plastic chair onto which he had dumped his bag. He had then fiddled around his waist, and his denim shorts dropped to his ankles. Fortunately, he had trunks on underneath; unfortunately, they were his fraying cotton ones. Clement had turned away as he slipped them off, and looked into Dirk's wide eyes as he returned.

'Dad!'

'I'm *desperate* for the loo,' the naked father had said to his son by way of greeting.

'What are you *doing*?'

'Your voice is cracking, my boy!' Dirk's dad had made his way to the back door. 'You're becoming a man!'

'Why don't you put on your cozzie while you're there?'

'I just have to go quickly. Not too long. You know your mother can smell where I've been. You know, like a dog.' The man then disappeared inside.

Clement kept his back to the house with

some effort. Although the sun had been clouded over for a while, the paving was still stinging hot. Clement hopped on one foot, then another: his slops were in Dirk's bedroom, but he wasn't venturing in that house with a naked man in it.

'I didn't think he was coming around today,' Dirk had said.

'Is it?'

'Ja. He's been… around. He doesn't have a phone on the boat, so he just pitches up. I'm sorry, man.'

'It's cool,' Clement said. Dirk had looked crestfallen, more so than usual. He hadn't mentioned any of this at school. Clement hadn't heard anything about Dirk's dad for a few years, certainly not since they were in senior primary, back when they had first become friends, when he first started coming around here. Even back then, Dirk's dad had already moved out, leaving behind his hi-fi system. Dirk didn't have TV games, but then again Clement could bring those around; more precious was the freedom Dirk had, yet seldom exercised. Sandy had supplied Dirk with a membership card for the rental shop, and they could put the sound up on the TV as much as they wanted. For Clement, this would be as loud as the system would go, but Dirk would always get stressed out, complaining the neighbours would get upset and call the police on them. But

Clement knew what Dirk was really scared of.

A flush had sounded from inside, and a series of doors slammed, the back door last of all. Instinctively, both boys turned around, only to be faced with a tanlined vision of manhood bouncing toward them, a can in hand. 'Hey, look what I found!'

'Dad, *no*!'

'It's just a *beer*. I've already had a couple.' He winked at Clement. 'What? Never seen balls before, Clem? Without these you wouldn't have your tjommie to play with.' He'd walked back to the plastic chair, and bent over it.

'*Dad*!'

Mercifully, Dirk's dad soon had his red lifesaver's trunks out of his duffel. Having settled himself into them, he then turned to the two boys, looked them up and down, and delivered his verdict. 'Thought I'd go for the record today. You may as well *both* help.'

Neither of them really had a choice.

Dirk came back with his dad's next beer just as the man resurfaced. Immediately the can was held out to him.

'No, not yet,' Dirk's father gasped, putting his hands on the wet caul of his hair. 'Let me finish my warm-up.' Five more breaths he sucked in and out, riblines expanding and striating at his flanks, before he sank back down under the surface.

The two boys watched him, again, cross-legged at the bottom of the pool, a small and steady stream of bubbles rising from his nostrils. Lazily, a dragonfly approached the surface, skimmed it, and departed.

'The fuck is he doing?' Clement said, finally.

'Holding his breath.'

Clement clapped Dirk on the back of his head. 'Ja, duh. I mean why?'

'It's his thing since he got the new boat. It's like a sport.'

'Like snorkeling?' Clement had gone snorkeling at Vetchies once before, but there were blue bottles, and he got stung on his foot before he saw anything good on the reef.

'No.' Dirk kept the beer in his hand as he crossed his arms. 'You just… hold your breath. Dad says you can swim while you do it too, but he's not ready yet.'

A second rumble sounded. The boys looked up to the sky. They heard a breath of wind before they felt it; a slight flight of air, tickling through the garden.

The father resurfaced again, this time scowling, lips pouting, and raspberried. He waded over to the side of the pool, eyes closed, his arm outstretched. 'Gimme that beer, son. Now.' Dirk did as he was told, and, fumbling for the ring pull, his father opened it, immediately pouring a foaming stream of it over his face. 'Jesus,' he hissed. He opened his eyes, blinking and wiping away the liquid, blinking again. 'Does your mother know I've been coming?'

'No.'

'You *sure*?'

'Ja.'

'Tell her to not put so much bloody HTH in here.' He poured some more beer over his face before finally putting it to his mouth. 'Jussie, jussie, jussie.' The beer scummed softly on the surface of the pool, then dissipated. The man looked at the boys, blinking again; Clement could see red creeping at the edges of his eyes.

'Don't you have goggles inside, Dirkie?'

'I don't know, Dad.'

'Don't you need them for PE? I remember I bought you some.'

'We don't do PE anymore, Mr Wilson.'

Dirk's dad turned to Clement. '*What*?'

'We're too old for it.'

'You *are*?' Dirk's dad burped as he made his way over to the pool's edge and put down the second beer. 'Well, Dirkie, could you have a look for me while I do my first dive?'

Dirk sighed as he walked back to the house. His father's eyes followed him. The man burped again, this time onto the back of his hand, the same hand he then used to free his watch from his wrist, offering it, dripping, to Clement. 'Time me two minutes, Clem. I can't keep my eyes open with this bloody chlorine. Just slap the water when it's done.'

'Ja, cool.' Clement looked at the watch as he took it. 'Hey, Mr Wilson, how can you see this underwater?' The face had a large LCD, but even so.

'Come on, Clem.' The man pushed off the wall back to the centre of the pool. 'You can train yourself to do anything, bru. You just have to push past the pain.' Theatrically he raised his arms above his head, and filled his lungs. 'Push past the pain,' he rasped as he relaxed his shoulders. 'Press the button when I go under, OK?' He looked to Clem. 'Two minutes, hey?'

'Sure.'

Dirk's dad then raised his arms again, lowering them in time with his breath, which grew deeper with each movement. Each lift of his muscled arms cast crescent wings of water, droplets that themselves flew and scattered back down onto the pool's surface. Faster the man's breath went, and further the arcs of water carried. Just when it seemed Dirk's father might have finally risen from the pool in flight, he dropped again to its bottom.

Clement pushed the start button on the watch, and heard its small beep. He exhaled then, realising he had been holding his own breath. Dirk's dad had resumed his usual meditative position; a small chain of pearls floated from him. Clement checked the stopwatch. Fifteen seconds. They went slowly when counted.

A low moan came from the sky just as the garden rustled again. This time it came from the bushes facing Clement, but they bore no mystery. Indeed it was a bird – a hadeda, patiently threading its overlarge body through the foliage onto the grass. It dipped its beak a few times into the lawn; finding nothing, it vented its wings and bellowed its way into the anonymity of the swaying canopy.

Dirk came back from the house then.

'Find the goggles?'

'No,' he grimaced.

'Why doesn't your dad get his own?'

'Dunno. He's always talking about money, so–'

The day flashed, and for an instant the entire garden was black and white.

'Whoa,' Dirk said, and sunk into himself. His hands clasped onto his ears, which Clement tried to pry away.

'Come on,' Clement muttered. 'Seriously, man.' Dirk was weak but determined, only relenting once he heard the thunder was over. 'Listen, bru, that was, like, a ten-second gap. It's ten kays away. At least.'

'But,' Dirk whimpered, 'it's coming *closer*.'

THE STORM

'Stop being a baby, man.'

'I can't help it. It's *loud*.'

Another flash, and Dirk cowered again. Clement counted in his head, watching his friend shiver. 'One-hundred-one, one-hundred-two, one-hundred-three,' he recited. At eight came the booming sound. Maybe it *was* coming closer, but maybe he was just counting wrong. If only he had a way to measure the–

'Shit,' Clement said, and looked at his wrist. The cycling numbers on the watch read two minutes twenty-something. 'Shit!' He ran back to the edge of the pool, and slapped the water with his open palm. It made a softer sound than he expected; nevertheless, Dirk's dad immediately surfaced, eyes closed, his mouth spraying a vapour that the wind blew into Clement's face.

'Sjoe,' Dirk's dad said, panting. 'That– was–' He paused to wipe his face. He opened his eyes. 'That was harder– than– I thought.' He waded toward the shallow end and put his dripping hands behind his dripping head. 'Sjoe. That was– two minutes– hey Clem?'

Clem nodded, stood, and began to wipe himself dry with the hem of his T-shirt.

'Sjoe, sjoe… sjoe.' Dirk's father coughed some kind of gelatinous substance into the water. 'I was counting– too– quickly.' He coughed again, regathering himself. 'OK, I guess that's why we train.' He whispered it to himself again. 'That's why we train, that's why we—' He coughed, and then spied his son, standing on the veranda, under the awning, as close as possible to the house, his hands clasped over his ears. 'What's his problem?'

'Scared of the thunder.'

The man's frown softened. 'Still?' With both his father and friend staring at him, Dirk put his hands down. 'Come on, son. I thought you'd grown up.' The sky flickered and Dirk clenched up again. Six seconds later came the thunder. 'You hear that,' his father called out, his breath steadier. 'It's ten kays away.'

'It's *loud*, Dad. I can't *help* it.'

'It can't *hurt* you, Dirkie.'

'It *can*!' Dirk calmed down. 'It can. There was a girl at our school who got hit by lightning.'

Dirk's dad looked at Clement. 'Really?'

'Ja, like… two years ago. She was standing under a tree.'

'You don't stand under a tree during a storm. Jussis.' Dirk's dad spat into the pool. 'Natural selection, hey.'

Clement laughed at that, as did the sky.

'OK, Dirkie, while you stand there being a little girl, me and Clem have some business to do.' He waded back to the middle of the pool. 'Three minutes this time, china.'

'Sure.'

Dirk's dad began his breathing again, raising and lowering his arms. Meanwhile, Clement fiddled with the watch until the timer cleared; he pressed the button when Dirk's dad shut his eyes and sank. He would watch time properly this time.

With his father submerged, Dirk called out to Clement. 'I'm gonna get some earplugs.'

'Kiff,' Clement chided, as Dirk flip-flopped to the back door. 'You can't find goggles but you'll find earplugs.' Dirk had his hands over his ears, though.

Left alone again by the poolside, Clement checked the watch, and then Dirk's dad. How still the man was, stiller than the water that engulfed him. Raindrops began to land with tiny ripples. They landed on Clement's arms, and the back of his neck – cool relief that his warm skin absorbed instantly. On the slasto the drops evaporated as they landed, to form clouds that would fall again as rain tomorrow. He then heard the slide and scuff of Dirk's slops, and turned to see his friend walking towards him with a ruff of toilet paper sticking out each of his ears. 'What the fuck, Dirk.'

'Huh?' He pulled one of the tufts of paper out. The end that came out of his ear held the shape of his ear canal, speckled with wax.

Clement scrunched up his face. 'What are you doing?'

'It works.' Dirk grinned as he reinserted it. It was the first time Clement had seen Dirk smile all day. He shook his head at his friend, but when the next roll of thunder came, Dirk didn't flinch. He did, however, look worryingly at the surface of the pool. 'Rain,' Dirk said. 'It's coming closer.'

Clement looked at the watch. Just over one minute gone. He turned back to Dirk, who was still looking into the pool, either at his father, or the bigger, slightly more frequent drops landing in it. Now the water began to settle on the slasto. A gust blew, and the leaves of the garden shimmered in the silvering light; from within them came the growing chatter of birds. The only still thing in sight was the tree that stood across the road, in the gap of the garden's canopy. A hadeda cawed, and Clement watched it land, clumsily, amongst that tree's upper branches.

Again Clement checked the watch. One minute thirty-something. The image of Dirk's father danced on the pool's surface. Clement gestured to Dirk to pull out one of his earplugs, which he did with some reluctance. 'Hey, why doesn't your dad practice in the marina?'

Dirk shrugged. A draught of cool air blew across the garden, unsettling some long-fallen leaves, blowing them into the pool.

'Have you ever gone on his boat?'

'*Obviously*. It's my *dad's*.'

THE STORM

'What's it like?'

Dirk thought for a moment before he replied. 'Small.'

'Oh.' Somehow that wasn't what Clement expected him to say. 'Have you stayed on it?'

'No. It's too small. There's like, nothing in it.' Dirk kept his eyes on his submerged father. 'Doesn't even have a sail.'

Another flash of lightning, and hurriedly Dirk bowed his head, stuffing the toilet paper back into his ear. Clement looked at the watch and timed it: after four seconds came a moan that reverberated in his chest.

It *was* getting closer.

As was, he realised, the three-minute mark. The rain came in bigger drops now, the sky closing in on them, drenching their cathedral of green, a vanguard of blue-grey cloud approached, banded in receding white. Clement could see the dark edges of anvil clouds, from which came a further spark and swift hammer blow. Clement motioned to Dirk.

'Bru!' he yelled over the percussion of water on slasto. 'Come get your dad out? I don't care how much chlorine's in the pool. Your dad's gobbed in it.' But Dirk just shook his head. He probably didn't even hear what Clement had said. By then there wasn't time to argue anyway. The three minutes had elapsed, and Clement slapped the surface of the water. It didn't make much noise over the rain, so he broke his fist through the surface with a gulp.

Dirk's father surfaced more calmly this time, as Clement wiped his hand on his dampening sleeve. The man wallowed toward the shallow end, and put his hands on his hips, bending over as the rain dripped down the back of his dripping head.

'Three– minutes– hey– Clem?'

'Ja.'

'That one–' He spat into the pool. 'Wasn't so– bad–. Counted it– right–' He exhaled. 'This time. Sjoe– Could– pace– myself– correctly.' He stood upright. Under the shade of his tan, his body was glowing red. He hocked into the pool, and looked up toward the sky. 'Rain's heavy. You're – getting soaked – there, Clem.'

Clement shrugged. 'I don't care.'

'Good – good boy.' He swallowed, and looked over to his son, who eyed him in turn. His arms folded, Dirk shuffled to the edge of the veranda, still under the cover of the awning, looking out toward the sky. He unstuffed one of his ears.

'*Dad?*'

'Ja?'

'Dad, I think you should come out.'

The man winced. 'I need to go for– for my best now– Dirkie.'

'Just until it goes past.'

THE STORM

'I'm all warmed up, Dirkie.'

'But the *lightning*.'

'I haven't seen any. It's just a bit of *rain*. Look, it's getting calmer now.'

And indeed, it was. The squall had let up, if only a little. The hadeda cawed again from its steady perch; Clement saw its silhouette proud against the pearlescent sky. The tree, the bird, so still. But maybe that was just because Clement had been watching them from afar: the garden around him still undulated, cupped leaves overfull with their catch, crying to the earth. 'There *is* lightning, Mr Wilson,' he said.

'Then I better get it over with quickly,' Dirk's father said. 'But first.' With a swift kick, he propelled himself over to the edge of the pool, and found his unfinished beer. The garden lit up just as he brought it to his lips. 'Ah!' He smiled, wiping his mouth. 'There's your lightning, boys!'

'Dad,' Dirk muttered, one last time, his hand hovering nervously around his uncovered ear. 'Please.'

As the man frowned, the can wrinkled in his fist. 'What, son? Are you scared?' 'Do you think *I'm* scared?' His lungs were strong; the words sprayed from his mouth. 'Where do you think I *fucking* sleep, son? If your *fucking* mother hadn't taken everything from me, I could have been training in the– the fucking *Bahamas* by now. Not that–' He burped. 'That fucking *cesspit* of a marina.' He raised the crumpled can to his mouth, and his head as he drank, his Adam's apple bobbing. He pointed at his son. 'Don't forget I *paid* for this pool, and that house. Even if I have to see your bitch mother,' he hissed, 'I will fucking *use* it.'

Dirk had stopped listening some time ago, though. The toilet paper reinserted, his eyes brimming, he had turned from his father and his friend, and started walking toward the back door.

'Still a baby.' His father watched him retreat before skulling the rest of the beer, and throwing the empty can where he had discarded his cigarette. 'Ag,' he sighed. For a moment Clement thought the man might go inside to comfort his son. Instead he just spat into the pool again. 'Beer's gone watery.' Beating the burps out his chest, he waded back once again to the centre. There he stood, in the midst of a hundred tiny waves. 'Ready, Clem?'

Clement nodded.

'OK then.' Dirk's dad puffed out his cheeks, and swung his arms around and behind his chest. He blinked, focusing his eyes straight ahead, at the darkened house. 'I'll come up when I have to, Clem. Just keep the time this time. My best is four minutes ten.' Dirk's dad restarted his breathing as the rain regathered its weight. Up went his arms,

THE STORM

and down, but having finished his usual routine, he paused. Arms raised to the sky, glistering chest inflated, he made chirping noises through pursed lips. He forced down his last sips of air into his body, until, finally, he went limp and dropped under the surface. Clement pressed the button on the watch.

The wind picked up again. Clement shivered. He looked at the pool, and everything that was suspended in it. The leaves, the foam, the man. At least he wouldn't have to touch any of it this time. Water fell into water, a static haze covering everything he saw, the white noise of sight and sound, until all the garden sounded its applause.

The world strobed around him, fluorescent, and Clement moved away from the edge of the pool to the veranda. Near the plastic furniture, where the stench of Dirk's dad's stale clothes overwhelmed the smell of rain, he took cover from the lashing, diagonal downpour. The metal awning dripped with rivulets down its every corrugation; the drumming on it produced its own sort of thunder. Except, no – *there* came the thunder. The garden illuminated again, and again two seconds later. Clement didn't count; there was no time to look at the watch before the boom and languid crackle.

The hairs on Clement's arms stood to attention, even through the damp. Cautiously, he stepped toward the pool, and peered into the broken and breaking surface. Dirk's dad sat at the bottom, as he expected. But as he continued to watch him, the man's legs slowly uncrossed, and drifted backward and away from his torso. Clement looked at the watch; he wasn't even halfway to his personal best, and yet the man looked like he might stand up at any moment. He didn't, though, and Mr Wilson's body rotated forward until it was almost horizontal, facing downward, his back slightly bent, his limbs hanging below him as anchors. The leaves that had been floating on the surface were sinking around him, the cloudburst breaking the surface into hundreds of tiny bouncing backjets; a dancing portal between dimensions. Clement squinted: was Dirk's dad–? No. Clement caught himself. If he looked carefully, he could just about see small bubbles rising and breaking directly above the man's head.

Clement recoiled before he knew exactly what he heard next. The next bolt of lightning hit and almost immediately filled his ears. Helplessly he crouched, his knees bending under him as he scrambled back to the veranda and braced himself on one of the plastic chairs. Keep low, he told himself. It will pass.

But something else was coming. A wetness slapped from somewhere behind Clement, and into the rain shower ran Dirk, his eyes wide and casting around the garden. Not seeing Clement on his haunches behind the chair, he ran through the new puddles to the pool's edge, calling his father. 'Dad!' he screamed. '*Dad!*' Through the surface he could see his father floating strangely, like a body down a river. Dirk screamed, and began to slap the surface of the water.

Clement stood up as straight as he could. 'He's fine, Dirk!' he hollered. 'Dirk!' He knew the man wouldn't hear his son over the disturbance of the rain, just as – Clement realised – Dirk couldn't hear Clement through his makeshift earplugs. Clement made to move toward Dirk, to pull him away – but as he stepped out from under the awning, Dirk jumped into the pool, fully clothed, directly onto the shape of his dad.

From one splash came another, as the two resurfaced together; immediately the father lashed out with his arms.

'Fuck, Dirk! *Fuck!*' The man's lungs were still very much full of air. Disoriented, however, he missed the first punch aimed at his son, and the second too. Dirk turned and fled toward the steps as his father lunged at him.

'I'm sorry!' Dirk cried. 'I'm *sor*-ry, Dad, please, I'm *sorry*.' But his red and light-headed father chased him as they exited the pool, water cascading from Dirk's clothes the same as if he had been standing in the rain the entire time. Growling his father pursued him to the first of a succession of doors that Dirk slammed on his way to his bedroom. His father rammed his shoulder into the back door, and stalked over the threshold of his old house.

Clement stood under the awning, listening to the storm coming from inside.

The torrent around him continued. The gutters burbled and overflowed, carrying sticks and detritus. The plants of the garden bowed to the force of the beating, the smacking unrelenting on the slasto, the driveway, the roof of the car parked on it. Vacated, the pool's level had risen, along with the only things left floating in it: two pieces of toilet paper, breaking up into pulp under the force of the rain. Clement wondered if it might overflow.

The world crashed in with a single beam of light, of light upon everything already lit, a colour beyond yellow, beyond white. The forked tongue of the sky appeared to Clement, and instantaneously disappeared, its afterimage burned on his sight as he fell, tripping backward onto one of the plastic chairs. At first Clement thought the lightning had hit the pool, but the blue stain on his vision receded toward its true target.

The lone tree in the other yard stood in its own bolt-shape, its bark split, as if something profound had been ripped out of it. He stared at it as his eyes came back into seeing, his ears into listening, his heart into motion. Clement blinked. The tree's upper branches were aflame. He blinked again. From the flames emerged a body of light itself, alight and alighting. As it vented its wings there came a further rumble from the sky, and after a moment, the bird was smothered in rain, and disappeared in a cloud of grey.

Clement sat, gripping the arms of the chair, not knowing what to do next. Instinctively, perhaps, he took a deep breath.

Comorbidities

Naomi Wood

FOR A WHILE, JOE had wanted to spice things up in the bedroom. 'If we don't make an effort now, there won't be anything left *to* improve,' he'd said, and though I knew he was right, I was also tired. I spent all of my time with the kids. His work was crazy. Even sex once a week was an effort, and sometimes when we got into bed its warmth simply overcame us.

When I thought about our lives, I thought about the therapy pie charts on the internet, divided into slices of time: like, here's your pie for work, pie for sleep, pie for kids. I knew our sex pie was so thin it could barely stand on its own. All of the websites said sex needed a bigger slice of the pie. They also said that if you don't have sex now, you can't have sex later – and I knew we couldn't stay on this minimal sex-percentage for ever, but we were tired! We were both so tired!

I used a lot of my pie on the kids. I think Joe

was a little jealous of my romance with Aida (6) and Casper (1). Often, I felt lovestruck by my babies. Joe was always having to pull me out of their beds because I'd fallen asleep, generally communing, amygdala to amygdala. Sometimes, it felt as if both babies were still inside me. I had read that the Y-chromosomes of boy foetuses have been found in the bones of dead mothers. Once they are inside you, they are inside you forever, sweeping through you with a Coriolis Force that went 'I love you/you drive me nuts/I love you/you drive me nuts' which would bore down to Australia before you got to the end, and besides, it always ended up with 'I love you', because that's the way it went with your kids.

This is how my love felt for Aida and Casper: bone-deep; viral.

A good chunk of my pie chart (like, maybe 8%) was also spent tracking the global melt of the polar ice shelfs according to the NASA website, which was a large percentage, particularly in comparison to the zero-point-something of our sex life. My ability to worry about anything was capacious, even profound, though I personally could not see how anyone slept at night, when floods, intensified storms, and freak supercanes were already bearing down upon us.

The other mothers at Rhyme Time could see it in me, this craziness, this relentless worry. They avoided me and talked with each other. I sang the nursery rhymes, but with very little heart. Sometimes I'd chat to them but it always ended up in eco-doom: 'Do you think our babies have a future?' I'd say. 'Will it be too hot to breathe?' But they did not want to think about our babies' extinctions. They wanted to sing 'Old MacDonald had a Farm', over and over, though the farm would be ashes, the animals charcoal, and the MacDonalds and their kiddiewinks burned in their beds.

When Aida started to ask about climate change, I levelled with her: 'It's all our fault,' I said, but mostly Granny and Grandad's: Cherry and Zhe-Shing, her ma ma and yeh yeh. Then Aida would run around butt-naked in the house screaming 'The world is on fire! The world is ON FIRE!' while Casper played with his new bottle, mauling the nipple with his teeth.

'Joe,' I once said, in the middle of the night. 'Do our kids have a future?'

'I'm asleep.'

'I know, but I'm scared.'

'You're always scared, whereas I have almost no opportunity to sleep.'

This seemed too good to have been made up on the spot. 'Did you practise that?'

'Maybe,' he said, rolling over, and I thought he really was asleep but then he said, 'You need to de-catastrophise. None of this helps the world.'

This is why I'm not horny! I wanted to say, the world on fire is not arousing! But in the morning I gave Joe a blowjob, as a way of saying sorry that I woke him, and sorry that our sex-pie was so thin. 'Thanks,' he said afterward. 'We needed that.'

Joe was a celebrity Mental Health nurse. Day in, day out, he was saving the lives of all the teenagers butchered by the internet: its hateful gossip, its rancorous memes, its 24/7 bullying. He listened to teenagers talk him through their suicide plans, and then carried that home. Sometimes I read his Twitter feed to see what he was feeling, to trace the graph's curve of years spent in the NHS (x) and his personal sense of failure to the kids he had lost in his high-security ward (y).

That morning, the morning of the BJ, he put out the stuff for breakfast and whistled as he went. I wondered: if I had chimerically morphed with the kids, had his brain become equally comorbid with his dick.

We heard through the kitchen the sounds of our neighbour Kelly and her daily panicked descant as she embarked on the school run. She had four kids. Four! I'd told her I could only have as many kids as I had hands. 'Otherwise they'd be raised by feet,' she'd said, looking with darkening anxiety into the kitchen. Kelly was also very tired, but she always listened with sympathetic absence to my thoughts on the planet.

Joe was right, though. My catastrophising wasn't helping. Aida's drawings showed the charred remains of lollipop trees, and when I looked at my babies there was a fiery orb around them, as if their aura re-circulated the cognitive blazes I privately envisioned. Joe had asked me to please not discuss this with his mother, because these conversations always went badly, but one day Cherry somehow embroiled me in the discussion.

'If I stop eating pork,' Cherry said, 'the world is not going to suddenly get better.'

Joe shot me a look. He had been at work for a long time; I could see the length of his shift in his face.

'No,' I said, 'but if *everyone* stopped eating pork it might.'

Casper kept on yanking at my bra. I was sure I still smelled of milk, though I had stopped breastfeeding weeks ago. Probably it was glandular. Maybe I was secreting it.

'Squeezy's so hungry,' she said, which was the name she used instead of Casper. She picked him up and settled him on her lap. 'Aren't you, baby?'

'Pigs fart,' said Aida. 'That's why the world's warming up.'

Cherry narrowed her eyes. 'I did not live

through decades of Communism to be told what to do here. If you've eaten boiled shoe leather, you notice the pork in your porridge. Aida, come here and count Squeezy's fat rolls.'

Joe's mother had hated our choice of name for Casper. Cherry had said it had supernatural connotations. ('Because of the Disney movie?' 'Uh-huh,' she said. 'Like the friendly ghost?' 'Uh-huh,' she said again.) Joe insisted his mother had a point, or at least that the point, however outlandish it seemed to me, was culturally sensitive. In Hong Kong, Joe said, there were massive holes in skyscrapers, like three apartments wide, for bad spirits to fly though – did I know how much that ancient suspicion could cost a real estate company? Ten of millions! Not letting ghosts into your house was worth tens of millions of dollars! Naming your child after a Disney ghost was just like inviting bad luck right into the crib.

But the real problem with Cherry was that she was always right about everything. She'd swum from Shenzhen to Hong Kong to escape Communism, waded through the Mai Po marshes at dawn – and that was in the day when you'd be shot if caught. But I put my foot down on the Casper front, insisted it was a name I had long cherished (who knows) and as a result Cherry always gave him less lai see than Aida at Chinese New Year, which was weird, because he was a boy, and, you know, etcetera…

'It's their future,' I said, emotional, 'that's why I'm concerned.'

'Hey,' said Joe. 'Are you crying?'

'I'm not crying.'

Since stopping breastfeeding I had felt very emotional. Perhaps I hadn't been ready, but Joe had this idea that when the baby was a year old it was time to let them go. In truth, while feeding Casper, I had never felt sure of my boundaries. There had been merge. Ontologically, I had felt synthesised. I'd loved it, and at the same time felt stranded by it.

'It's the milk,' said Cherry, 'it's coming out of your eyes.'

'It's not the milk coming out of my eyes.'

Cherry looked at me and crossed herself. She had hedged her bets, and was now both a Taoist and a Baptist. 'If you have another baby,' she said, 'then you can feed that one too. Joe said you're sad about stopping.'

'I'm not sad. I'm fine.'

Cherry desperately wanted us to have a third child. Perhaps it was because she herself had had only one.

'There are already too many people in the world,' I said.

'Nonsense.' She looked at Joe. 'Poor Joe, you look so tired. Why don't I take Squeezy too next

Saturday?' she said, actually winking. 'When was the last time you were by yourselves? You can have a date night!'

'I don't think so,' I said, before Joe could agree. 'Squeezy can take the bottle now.'

'That would be wonderful,' said Joe, before I could offer another protest.

When Cherry had gone, Joe cracked open a beer. Caspar was threatening to run a black crayon up the wall. When I took it off him he started to cry, then attacked Aida, clawing at her face. Then Aida tripped him over, and his wails filled the room.

'Enough!' said Joe. 'Time for bed! Everyone!'

'It's four o'clock,' I said.

'Then why aren't we watching TV?' he said. 'And no *Topsy and Tim*, okay? That shit has very toxic gender roles.'

I thought about what a good mood he had been in after the blowjob and how he hadn't whistled for weeks. As we settled on the sofa, I said, 'How about a home movie on Saturday night?'

'Sure,' he said, laughing, as Topsy made cupcakes with Mummy, and Tim drove his toy 4x4 across the savannah of their astroturfed garden. 'See you there, Ms Kardashian.'

About seven bajillion years ago, Joe and I met on

a dating app dominated by aggressively randy men. I'd been sent tons of dick pics, which sometimes made me feel horny and sometimes grossed-out. Sometimes I got into extended sexting conversations where I'd take nude pictures of myself and they'd send laughably priapic photos, which I'd then Reverse Google Image Search to see if they had been cribbed from the internet. Sometimes we'd have phone sex which would end with an insane orgasm but also the astral distance of strangers who didn't love each other, who didn't know each other, who didn't even know if the other's profile photo was real; though sometimes it was this very nothingness that made the exchange so arousing, like having sex with a zero, or a bot, or yourself.

Any hope of a relationship was useless. It was like whamming your head into the crotch of all these dudes, giving 800 blowjobs, and asking for nothing back, and I knew the delinquency was only a front to hide my inner, terrible longings for intimacy.

So when I started messaging Joe I found his sincerity almost anti-normative. As a public-facing Mental Health nurse, he had half a million Twitter followers @PoetParamedic. He had warned me, over the app, that he was Chinese, like *fully* Chinese, and that when some white women met him they were disappointed. He was in turn surprised when, at the tail end of our first date, he found me so wet for him. Suddenly, at 27, I had felt for the first time the total vortical tension of falling in love, and I remembered with some regret the austerity of all those unnumbered dudes with whom I'd done so many nothings, so many times.

Joe was quieter than the other guys I'd dated, and a thousand percent more sensitive. Often, when I fucked up, like when he was recording a live segment for TV at home, and the kids swarmed into the living room as I was scrolling Instagram in the kitchen and didn't notice after five – then ten minutes – he was more or less instantly forgiving. He lived with the theory that with no ill-will there was never any responsibility; the kids he worked with were proof of this. Given world history, I personally thought this was a bad argument, but it was one I accepted.

The next Saturday we packed Aida and Casper off to Cherry's. We would reunite for Sunday lunch at Jade Garden, but for the next 24 hours, both kids were gone. Instead of being anxious, as I thought I would be, I felt joyful. There was a sense of festivity in the house, as if we were both on holiday.

I told Joe that I had great things planned for

us, sexually, on our first kid-free morning, but in the meantime, we would sleep. We hadn't slept through the night for twelve months, and that night we slept cadaverously and without interruption. When we woke there was actual daylight peeping at the curtains, and we marvelled at the fact that nobody needed anything from us.

For a while I looked at Joe's body; the sexy line of hair from his navel to crotch, his slender frame which hid his strength. When he was in his scrubs he looked even better because I could see the faint outline of his penis, which seemed, to me anyway, like a failure in tailoring. I kissed him on his chest. I could tell he was close-eyed-thinking rather than sleeping. I whispered: 'Do you want to make that movie?'

He opened his eyes. 'I thought you were joking.'

'Why not?'

I could tell he was surprised. For most of my pregnancy and Casper's life, I had stopped initiating. I knew it frustrated him that I no longer wanted him like he wanted me. He understood – we both understood – that our inability to care for one another was because our burden of care was so large – but it didn't mean he wasn't sad that this part of us had so quietly died; a part of us that had once been so raw and lurid.

'We've got to be careful,' he said. 'Paris

Hilton… Kim Kardashian.'

'Weren't they on purpose? Didn't they actually release them?' I shifted onto my back as he played with my nipple. 'Also Hulk Hogan.'

'Hulk Hogan what?'

'He released a tape.'

'Did he?' He scrunched up his nose. 'Gross.'

Joe abandoned my nipple and read a blog about digital security and home movies, then went downstairs to fiddle with his laptop: turning off the Cloud, putting his searches on private, clearing his cache and browser history, then turning his phone onto airplane mode.

He was right to be paranoid. A few years ago, his Twitter account had been hacked, and the hackers had taken Thai Ladyboy faces and pasted them onto pictures of him they'd found in his iPhotos, with racist captions in shadowbox lettering saying things like 'Yin Yang, suck my dang'. Otherwise he got sent messages saying 'Why dont u kill urself', or a pasted menu from a Chinese takeaway, or they'd send videos of themselves wanking during his Teen Mental-Health slot on CBBC.

When Joe came back he put his phone on the pillow, flipped the viewfinder and toggled to video. I wondered if I should have tidied my bush but it was too late now.

'Are you sure everything's off?'

'Sure.'

'We're not on Instagram Live?'

'No.' He showed me the phone's aeroplane mode. 'Imagine we're inside the plane, 40,000 feet from the world, our family, the kids.'

Knowing I could kybosh this whole thing with my anxiety, Joe started kissing me, and slowly I began to switch off my worries. At first, we couldn't look at each other without laughing. But when I watched the video I stopped thinking. It was pretty hot. I was turned on by Joe's lips and the way they were mashed by my own. When he took off my T-shirt I watched as his lips moved the nipple around, kissing and licking me.

Casper had favoured the right boob, and it was noticeably bigger than the left, but I tried not to think about the kids. I had wondered if I would feel weird about my post-pregnancy body, but it looked okay: the boobs had more sag, there was a cradle of fat hip to hip, but mostly it was fine. Joe's body was still pretty much the honeymoon it was in his twenties, which wasn't fair, but it was at least mine to enjoy.

Joe sat me on top of him. In the video we watched ourselves intensely, which might have proved monotonous but was very arousing. We came quickly, and I pressed the red button immediately to stop the recording.

We cuddled, then Joe went to the bathroom.

When he came back he twinned his phone to Bluetooth, and I listened to the lonely submarine pulse of the speaker trying to find its pair. He began a mellow playlist I hadn't heard in a while. Soon I realised it was the playlist he'd made for the birth of Casper, though he must have forgotten this. A Brian Eno song began playing, and Caspar's labour came back to me: the abrasion; burn; rip; a flow of blood; then everything went dark, as if I had died – but instead a baby was placed on my chest; a heavy thing with a mineral stench.

Joe was sleeping now. Over the song I heard the rhythmic loop of the bathroom's extractor fan. I felt a little sad. The sex had been nice, kinky; a return to form. It had a lustiness we'd once taken for granted. But something in me felt empty. Only now that the kids were away did I realise how much we had both lost, the price we had paid. I thought I was about to cry, but instead I saw Casper's breast begin to gently leak milk against the pillow.

The windows of Jade Garden were tinted, as if to ward off great shelves of subtropical light, and inside the air was hostile with air-conditioning. On some tables there were pristine cloths and spotless Lazy Susans; on the tables recently vacated, a general wreckage of tea-leaves, bones, towers of dim sum crates, and the general atmosphere of a raid. Through the aisles older women pushed trollies, picking up empties as they went.

When I saw my children, sitting nicely for their ma ma and yeh yeh, I felt things which were hard to admit. I wanted to preserve who I had been this morning, and not go back to being these good people of endless patience and infinite care. I looked at Joe, panicked, not wanting to say goodbye. He kissed me. I guess he was thinking the same thing. Then we went over to them: our old frontier.

Zhi-Sheng's nose ruffled when I kissed him hello. Even with the faintly aquatic smell of prawn in the air, I could still smell the bedsheets on us. He was filling in the dim sum docket. 'Are you still vegetarian?' he asked.

'Pescatarian.'

'What's that?'

Joe placed his phone on the table provocatively. I looked at it and looked at him. 'Only seafood,' he said. 'And fish.'

'What's the point in that?'

'Fish don't fart,' said Aida.

'Exactly,' I said, putting her on my lap. I looked at the outline of Aida's face, and the fineness of her features, her overwhelming beauty.

'Can we play "Silly Lady"?' she whispered.

Aida loved playing 'Silly Lady'. It involved me pretending I had absolutely no idea who she was, and that I had to take her to a police station in order to find her real mummy. It only worked if we played it in public – that was the point – there was a longing in her to feel publicly disowned, which might, I guess, be universal. Often she went berserk, saying 'Mummy! Mummy! It's me!' as she jumped into my eyeline, but I would disavow all knowledge of her, and one time she had laughed so hard she had wet herself, as if her bladder could not handle the queasy uncertainty of not being mine.

'Not now, darling,' I said.

'Did you profit from the morning?' asked Cherry, a glint in her eye.

'We just watched a movie,' said Joe, suppressing a smile. He tapped his phone with a finger. 'We'll probably watch another one later, too.'

'Squeezy was so cute. He filled diaper after diaper! When are you going to potty train him?'

'Next summer,' said Joe.

Crates of dumplings arrived: rosebuds of siu mai, winter melon bao, and some wonton that Cherry scooped out for Casper. As I watched Zhi-Sheng dunk his bun in soy sauce, turning its milky whiteness the colour of wood stain, I realised I was ravenous. Everything Cherry put on my plate, I ate; even the chicken feet. Zhi-Sheng said something in Putonghua, which I guessed was 'I thought she was pescatarian' and Joe just shrugged, and smiled at me for miles.

Zhi-Sheng had to order more. He had a long conversation with one of the trolley ladies while Cherry visibly yawned; he was always flirting with the waitresses, getting a little drunk, and flushing with beer.

Aida put one of the bamboo crates on her head, and said, 'Look, I'm ma ma when she was a peasant!' and I swatted the crate away before Cherry could see. More food was brought. Because of the video, and the energy I'd put into it, I felt so hungry. On and on I ate, and I thought: I could do this all day. I could do this all day!

'Are you pregnant?' Cherry said quietly.

'Ha, ha, ha,' I said, through a mouthful of dumpling. 'Ha, ha, ha.'

'You know, I couldn't conceive in Shenzhen. All that sweet stuff in Hong Kong – the dan tat, the peanut butter pancakes! – that's finally what made Joe.'

'Or maybe you were less stressed?' I said, eating the chicken foot the way I had learnt from her, with my lips closed and my mouth labouring. I extricated the bones, and said: 'I can't imagine the shoe factory was very… nourishing?'

For years Cherry had made knock-off Michael Jordans at a factory in Shenzhen that specialised in perfect counterfeits. She returned my gaze. 'No. Freedom did it.'

'How was church?' I asked Aida.

'A man was in the water and another man had to pull him out!'

'He made such a loud noise!' said Cherry. 'So dramatic! Like he was drowning. You're meant to fill in the form if you can't swim.'

'I can swim,' said Aida, with some expectation.

'You can wait till you're eighteen,' I said.

The language went Putonghua, and I tuned out, tranquilised by the MSG, and happy to remove myself from the grown-up conversation. Repetitively I fetched whatever morsel Casper threw to the floor; Joe watched Aida spin his phone on the table. I finished off the food, while Casper had a meltdown, struggling with his strong limbs to get out of the high-chair, and nearly knocking it over, and smashing his face in.

I imagined us in the famous scene from *Don't Look Now*, where Donald and Julie have sex, intercut with their musing about it afterward. In my reconception, it was with two spacey parents responding to their children in the restaurant, cut into the sex scene. And the audience would think: haven't they done enough! Don't they deserve a longer break!

I looked over at Joe, who was also lost in thought. I wondered if intimacy was fleeting, or whether you had to constantly re-make it. Most of my friends thought I was lucky to be in love with my husband after kids. A friend's husband now actually slept in a toddler bed, because their youngest boy would howl 'I'm lonely, I'm lonely!' in the night, and they'd dozily swap places at three in the morning. So yes, I felt lucky, but also…

I looked at the bones on the table. What had I done? Why had I eaten all this animal? I shivered. I felt crazy, and unlike myself. Maybe I was doped up on sex, or MSG; the mood felt fugue-like, and not unwelcome. There was an air freshener a little way off, and I tried to pace how long it took to spray its pine scent.

'Joe,' I said, and he turned to look at me, but I didn't have anything to say, and he took my hand, and Cherry nodded to herself, as if in confirmation. The table was now clear.

'I'm glad you've broken the curse.'

'She's not pregnant, Ma,' said Joe, exasperated. 'We told you. No more babies.'

'Why not? Look at Squeezy!'

We all turned to look at him. With all the attention on him Casper beamed, then leant over and bit me with his hard ridged gums.

'Two is enough,' Joe said, as I pried Casper off me.

'Two is no better than a pair.'

I didn't know what this meant.

'Cherry's always been baby-mad,' said Zhi-

Sheng. 'That's why she loved Joe too much.'

'You can't love a baby too much,' I said.

'Yes, you can,' Zhi-Sheng said, and then he watched his wife, to see how she would react.

After lunch we went to Hyde Park. Joe went ahead with the pushchair and his dad, while Aida walked with me and Cherry. The day was bright and glossy, and the trees, heavy with blossom, were shook by mild winds. The heavy refrigeration of Jade Garden was beginning to thaw, and all the cultivated nearness of the restaurant had dropped away.

'Is Joe OK?' said Cherry.

I knew it took a lot for Cherry to ask me this. 'His work is exhausting,' I said. 'The caseloads are bigger. The work is more complex.'

'We could take them on a Friday night too?'

'Then he just wouldn't ever see the kids.'

She nodded. 'I show the ladies at Bridge the videos of him on TV. They're so jealous, but they don't even know how tough it is for him.'

'It's hard.' Though I knew she wouldn't understand, I wanted someone to talk to. 'We say: here's the internet!' I gestured to an imaginary esplanade. 'Poke around, kids, but it's like a dungeon in there? Rape porn, bullying, one-dollar bikinis' – I counted them on my fingers – 'beheadings, hacking, child abuse – often from each other. I mean. This is what he listens to. This is what is on his mind *all the time.*'

Cherry nodded but looked vacant. We passed the Peter Pan statue with the rabbits and children coming from the black rock, and I thought of our neighbour Kelly, with her kids swarming her skirts. 'I grew up in a village,' she said. 'I have no idea.' Cherry looked at the sculpture plangently, as if it hid all the children she had never had. 'So you're not pregnant?'

'Nope.'

We carried on to the Serpentine. The light had a satiny bounce off the water, and Cherry popped on her Ray-Bans, which made her look fantastic. 'I never liked her,' she said tartly as we reached the Memorial Fountain.

'Princess Diana?'

'What a whiner. If I was a princess, I would have enjoyed myself!'

Joe and his dad had already crossed the river, and I saw Cherry gaze at them fondly. In the pushchair Casper had nodded off, his absurd curls crowning his big forehead. Zhi-Sheng waved and blew a kiss; maybe the amatory result of the lunchtime beers.

Aida ran over to the bridge. As I watched her, I thought of our video in the future, joining the deadly slime of the internet that had made all those teenagers' lives miserable. The thought of someone leaking the video onto some democratic porn hub made my face burn. Imagine if the kids, one day, found it, and watched it! I thought of Joe touching the airplane mode to show me his phone was off. When he'd done that, had he accidentally turned it on again? I felt intensely panicked, and texted Joe on the other side of the river: *delete the video*.

I saw him look at his phone. Three dots appeared as he wrote back.

The air had gone gummy and chilled, and a wind gusted through the trees. I turned, looking for Aida, who was now up on the bridge. She couldn't see me, but I could see her. Over here! I wanted to say, the Coriolis Force barrelling through me. Aida, Aida, I love you! While we were in the shade, she was in the last of the sun – and the radial flames tore around her head.

Guests

Cherise Saywell

NATALIE KNEW THE MATTER of the fence wasn't finished. Tall and slatted, scabbed with lichen, it marked the boundary with the place next door. You could see through the gaps to the exterior of the house, which had been renovated in the colonial style, painted a warm biscuit tone, olive-green banisters, a dark red roof. There was an arbour planted with cuttings, and beyond that, a pool. Sometimes Natalie and her boyfriend Kurt liked to swim there – the owners turned the outside lights off when they were away.

Natalie's own place, shared with Kurt, was a subdivision with a flimsy partition wall, on the other side of which lived Bilen. Just after dawn, Natalie had found her crouched by the fence holding a rock in her hand. She must have been hitting it against the slats – the noise broke into the early morning stillness. Bilen had made no apology, said nothing at all, simply got to her feet, watching Natalie's face, and Natalie couldn't remember if she'd favoured one leg as she rose. Now here she was, nine hours later, mid-afternoon, standing on the back veranda by the door. It was as if she knew Natalie would be waiting. A calico bag hung over her arm and she held a shallow pan in her hands. Nestled inside the pan was a gas burner. Her little boy was counting each of the four steps that led off the veranda as he leaped down into the yard.

'Please come with me,' Bilen said to Natalie.

It was a shock to hear her voice. Through the partition wall, everything was audible, all the comings and goings: complaints, disturbances, once even a police raid, this neighbour removed along with his hydroponic marijuana crop. Before Bilen the tenants next door were the kinds of people who couldn't keep their trouble to themselves. They stayed only briefly, and then left, or were removed. Bilen was a different sort of trouble, Natalie thought, so quiet as to seem barely present, soundless on the other side of the wall, and soundless crossing the veranda to the yard where she hung her laundry. Her rent was paid by a charity – the landlord had informed Natalie of this (he liked to collect hers weekly, in cash.) She was from Ethiopia? Eritrea?… Natalie couldn't remember… Something about a war. Apparently, she had shrapnel in her leg. *Shrapnel*

– the word had snagged in Natalie's mind, the idea of metal buried in flesh. Still, she couldn't help feeling Bilen's silence implied a certain lightness – as if her tenancy was a stop along the way to somewhere better.

Bilen turned now and walked along the veranda and Natalie followed her, feeling an odd mix of discomfort and resentment, wondering what the burner and the pan were for.

'Sit here,' Bilen said, indicating the steps that led down as if Natalie were a guest, but Natalie didn't react, just perched at the top, under the awning. There was no shade in the yard; the air was bleached and still, the sky a bright, hot stone. Grass grew only sparsely, in long knotted strands. Bilen, apparently oblivious to the heat, set the gas burner on the paving and shook out a cloth boldly patterned in maroon and orange. She tucked one leg beneath her body (surely not the injured one?) and stretched the other out in front. They might be the same age, Natalie thought. Bilen's features suggested youth. But her clothes, faded in the way of the much-worn and often-washed – today, a pink blouse embroidered around the collar, a wrap-around skirt with a hibiscus print – were of a style Natalie would never wear, nor anyone her age she knew. She couldn't imagine Bilen dancing in a club or at a gig, or mixing drinks at a party. There was her little boy too – he was perhaps four or five years old. But it was more than all these things – something about the way she carried herself – as if she had no time for the trivialities that preoccupied Natalie.

Bilen balanced the pan on the flame, moved her hand back and forth over it. When satisfied with the temperature, she dropped in a handful of green pellets, which clattered over the metal surface. She said nothing as she did this, didn't even catch Natalie's eye, though she occasionally checked her little boy who had circled the perimeter of the yard and now paused to peer through the gaps in the fence. From where he stood, the pool would be visible, tiled in a pale powder blue with a darker mosaic around the edge, occasional shifts in the air trailing fragments of broken light across the surface of the water. The boy turned and locked eyes with Natalie. He paddled his arms wide around his body, and Natalie wondered if he had come here in a boat with Bilen, down through Indonesia like the refugees in the 1970s. Or maybe they'd flown. Natalie had travelled here on a bus, with Kurt, crossing hundreds of miles of semi-arid plains, haze of dust, sun setting red, enough cash to pay for ten nights in a hostel while they searched for work. It had been her idea to come to the city. Five years out of school and she'd gone nowhere, done nothing, just worked in the local newsagent, ringing up sweets and cigarettes and magazines, counting out change, and only the weekends to look forward to. They'd been lucky to find this flat so quickly, lucky to have enough money to move in. Kurt joked to his friends back home that they'd got themselves a place with a pool.

Soon, all the green in the pan was gone. The pellets had darkened to a glossy brown, glistening with an oily sheen, their roasted scent familiar. On her way to the cinema where she now worked as an usher, Natalie passed a row of coffee shops, some with grinding machines in their service area. She'd pause to breathe the rich air. But those cafes were so expensive. She got her coffee from the dispensing machine in the foyer, which was discounted to staff.

Bilen tipped the beans onto a woven mat, fanning them with the lid from the pan. When they had cooled, she lifted the mat and moved it gently, rolling and turning the beans.

'Good, yes?' she murmured, leaning towards where Natalie sat, on the step. She looked into her eyes when she said this, and Natalie felt herself smile.

'Yes,' she agreed.

Bilen did not smile, but nodded once, then put the mat down and removed a packet of popping corn from her bag. Her little boy ran over as if she had signalled to him. He scooped a handful of kernels and dropped them into the pan. She covered it, returned it to the flame, but before the corn began to pop there came a sudden splash – someone entering the pool next door. The boy jumped up and ran again to the fence, pressed his face to a gap, seeking, Natalie supposed, a view of the swimmer. She thought of how the water would feel. She and Kurt had used the pool only last night. The exterior lights had been out for several days, the driveway empty. It was so warm they didn't bother about towels and because it was late and there was no one about, they'd removed their clothes in the yard, leaving them in a careless heap. Kurt had loosened some nails near the back corner in the spot they always used – 'the gate', he liked to call it. Naked and silent they'd lifted the slats and crawled through the gap emerging among the shrubbery. They did not splash at all when they entered the pool. The water parted itself around their bodies; the darkness made room for them.

The boy craned his neck now and apparently dissatisfied with the view, slipped his hands into a gap, gripped one of the slats, but Bilen called to him, saying something first in their own language, then in English: 'Come away, child, come away.'

She extinguished the flame and removed a

mortar and pestle from her bag. She poured the beans into the mortar and began to grind them, rotating the bowl, moving the pestle into the base in a sort of whirling and pressing motion. She leaned in, angling her back, shifting a little more heavily to her right, and Natalie pictured the shrapnel as she imagined it would look on her own body – a scattering of something fragmented, barbed and buried, but visible on the surface in shades of stormy blue, or blackish green. She settled her gaze on Bilen's left leg and in her reverie, she pressed at her own thigh. A deep blush warmed her face when Bilen caught her staring, but Bilen averted her gaze, gave her attention to the burner instead – cool now – she put it into the bag, the pestle too. She shook out the cloth and draped it over her shoulder.

'We will go inside to prepare the coffee,' she said to Natalie.

She hooked the bag over her arm, collected the pan with its cargo of corn, then with her free hand she lifted the mortar containing the coffee. 'Come, come,' she called to her little boy.

He followed them along the veranda.

They entered Bilen's flat through her kitchen. The work surface was bare and the bedroom they passed, off the hall, contained only a pair of rolled-up mats with a neat mound of folded clothing beside each. The living room was almost entirely unfurnished but for a wooden chair by the window and several brocade-covered cushions. The carpet — a trodden shade of green, the same as in Natalie's flat — bubbled up where the floorboards were uneven. On a shelf that was fixed to the wall were several books in a foreign script, and a dictionary of English. Natalie had furnished her own living room within days of moving in. The previous tenant had left a beanbag and an ancient television. Kurt had got a dark green sofa from a workmate in exchange for a baggie. And she'd hauled a coffee table back from a secondhand shop. Now, Kurt displayed his bong collection on the coffee table. He had three, all made of glass, which he cleaned after every use. He'd brought them from home in his suitcase, protected with wads of tissue paper and layers of bubble wrap. In high school, Kurt had been known for his improvised smoking devices, his best an apple with a mouthpiece cut in, a separate but connected opening carved and lined with a foil cone. The *hash pash*, his friends would laugh when he fitted his lips to it and lit up. Even now it was his catchphrase, his claim to fame.

Bilen seemed unaware of the sparseness of her living room. She put out three of the cushions and shook open the cloth. In here, its colours seemed more vivid; it appeared to float on the surface of the ugly carpet. She situated the gas burner in the middle. Her little boy fetched three napkins from the shelf, then he climbed up on the chair at the window from where, standing behind him, Natalie could see the entire length of the pool next door. The swimmer, a man wearing bright red trunks, was floating on his back, arms out, kicking his legs gently. How visible would she and Kurt have been, had Bilen watched from here? But it had been late – after eleven – and dark, and they'd been very quiet, taking with them only a plastic milk bottle, its bottom section cut away. Kurt had modified it with a short length of transparent tubing and taped their dope, wrapped in a rag of foil, to the side. One toke each. 'We'll do them like bucket bongs,' he'd said, 'but in the pool.' After their swim, they'd sat at the shallow end, on the steps, the water encircling their waists. Kurt went first and then Natalie took her turn, lighting the cone, mouth over the open top of the bottle, leaning forward and pushing it into the water to force the smoke up, channelling it deep into her lungs. She'd coughed and then everything slowed and softened as if dialled down to a lower setting.

Next door, the swimmer climbed out of the pool now and strode onto the grass; the water swilled and rippled where he had been. His wet skin glistened and sunlight caught him at certain angles, sharpening his outline. He threw a towel over a deckchair and lay down. The boy watched him closely, then he turned and addressed Natalie. Enunciating each word with great care, he said, 'Somebody is swimming in your pool.'

Natalie's vision fuzzed, her mouth felt cottony and dry. 'Swimming in *the* pool,' she said, a little too loudly. 'Not *my* pool.'

'He likes to look at it,' Bilen said, 'how the tiles colour the water. He is excited he can see the bottom.' She seemed to hesitate, and Natalie thought she might say something more, but she abruptly turned and left the room returning moments later with a tray; on it three small ceramic cups, a bowl, a jug of water, a spoon, a packet of plain sweet biscuits, and a metal pot. The pot had been fashioned from tin cans. Natalie recognised the characteristic ridging, and the base was unaltered – if you took a can opener to it, it would fall neatly away. But the body had been widened and shaped with additional strips of tin. Despite the crude soldering, its tapered shape, deeply curved handle, and long spout lent it a kind of elegance.

'Did you make it?' Natalie asked, coming closer, reaching out to touch.

'My friend did,' Bilen replied. 'A *jebena,* for cooking the coffee.'

'*Jebena*,' Natalie repeated, feeling the shape of the word in her mouth.

Bilen nodded to herself, as if remembering. 'We were soldiers together. When there was a safe time, I cooked the food from the tins, and we ate. Then my friend cut them...' She made a hissing sound, pointed one finger, '...and joined the metal... My good fortune.' She nodded slowly, as if pleased at the memory. 'Now I can make the coffee in the best way.'

She poured water from the jug, then spooned in the coffee she had ground. She sat the *jebena* on the burner and lit the flame.

While the coffee cooked, she tipped the popcorn into a bowl. The boy settled himself beside his mother and she held out a packet of biscuits from which he counted six, arranging them carefully in a floret on top of the popcorn. When this was done, he reached for the packet again, but he watched his mother's face as he did this, as if anticipating what she would do. She smiled and said something to him in their own language, perhaps asking him to wait, or to be patient, for he didn't fuss, only sighed.

Natalie returned to the window, gazed out at the pool again. Last night she and Kurt had almost been caught, each moment overtaking the next: light slicing the darkness as the car turned into the drive, that brief silence after the engine cut, doors opening and closing, voices. They'd slunk out of the water, slid into the shadows beyond the arbour, then they'd gone through the fence, lifting the slats back into place, after which Kurt had darted across the yard ahead of Natalie, using the bong to protect his modesty. He'd leaped up the stairs, treading along the veranda in exaggerated tippy-toe steps as if making himself light. The boards groaned beneath his weight in a way that made the whole business seem comical now that they were safely on their side of the fence. Natalie had snorted, almost laughing out loud. She'd clapped her hand over her mouth to contain herself, and then crouched down to pull on her dress. This was the moment she realised that someone had witnessed their trespass after all, for their clothes were not in a flung-down heap as they had left them. Comprehension arrived in a chill rush, settled into a kind of cold clarity, and then something else, because it was hard to make sense of exactly what was being communicated. Each garment had been folded and left in an odd little row – her dress, Kurt's shorts and his shirt, even their underwear – like a sort of sentence, Natalie thought, saying what? A warning maybe, that Bilen might inform the landlord, or that she might tell the neighbour, for that matter. But this possibility didn't seem real. It merely floated through Natalie's mind and then sank. She'd dropped her dress over her head, thinking of the row of folded clothes as… not a reproach exactly, but a judgement. She'd gathered up Kurt's things, shaking them out and talking herself into indignation. It was nobody's business what they did; they'd caused no harm.

Inside, she'd said nothing to Kurt. They'd watched some television and smoked a little more, but the drug did not sedate her. Nor could she nurture her indignation; instead, a new feeling crept up on her. She pictured herself as if from a distance, sitting, ghostly, in a cloud of filthy bongwater at the shallow end of that beautiful pool, then crawling naked through the fence, creeping across the yard. After this, she saw herself at work, watching the same film from the retractable seat in the back corner for a fourth, fifth, sixth time; after each screening, inching forward over the floor, bending down to prise loose sweets that had been trodden into the carpet; tying the bin-bag, hands sticky from picking up popcorn, paper cups and plastic lids; then walking home, past the coffee shops, closed now, past the plate-glass windows of the boutiques on Elizabeth St, the mannequins with their glassy lips, their polished eyes and brittle limbs, wearing the sorts of clothes you could dance in at a concert or a gig, or when mixing drinks at a party. She'd been here almost a year and she'd done none of these things, and the only people who visited were a couple of Kurt's friends from work, men who liked to smoke with him.

Natalie squeezed her hands together and blinked hard, stared into the carpet, and when she felt ready to look up again, Bilen was removing the lid from the *jebena*, checking the contents.

'Sit down,' she said to Natalie, beckoning, and Natalie did.

The boy rose from where he had crouched keeping watch over the biscuits, and he moved closer to his mother. She patted the rug, indicating that he should settle himself, but before he sat, he smiled at Natalie and paddled his arms around his body again like he had in the yard. He sat then, and tried again, this time leaning as if floating on his back, but in doing so he lost his balance and reached for his mother's leg to save his fall, catching instead the hem of her skirt. Bilen was holding the *jebena*, and so had only one hand with which to rescue him, and this she did, but still he dragged her skirt sideways and up, revealing above her left knee a raised ridge of scar tissue, discoloured, irregular in shape, as if something hot had been poured there and hardened quickly.

It was nothing like what Natalie had imagined.

Dimly she was aware that this was an accidental exposure and that the right thing to do was to look away. Or to help – her hands were empty; she might have taken the *jebena*, or even the weight of the boy.

But she was recalling that vision she'd had of herself in the pool and crawling naked through the fence. She was remembering how her stomach had dropped at the sight of those folded garments, how she'd felt as if she'd exposed something more than her body. She didn't want to be cruel, rather, she hoped to sound magnanimous, or generous, or considerate, she wasn't quite sure. She heard herself speak. 'Would you like this cushion?' she asked, lifting the one she was sitting on, 'So that your leg doesn't hurt.'

Bilen was not unkind, but she regarded Natalie like a creature that had somehow tried to speak when its throat had not yet evolved to form the words.

'Thank you,' she said, 'there is no need.'

She put the *jebena* on the tray and spoke softly to her son. He sat up and she lifted his hand and put it to her lips, looking into his face, while with the other she adjusted her skirt, smoothing the fabric back into place. None of this was hurried, but it proceeded in a matter of seconds, as if Bilen had moved everything smoothly forward, past the awkward moment.

Now she took a twist of cloth from her bag and unwrapped it: inside it, a lump, like resin, a dark tobacco colour. She placed a small metal dish on the burner and broke off a piece of the resin. When she dropped it in, a pale fragrant smoke was released, the scent spiced and woody – frankincense, maybe. Bilen uttered a blessing in her own language. 'Now we can drink the coffee,' she said. She poured it into two cups, some water for the boy in a third.

The coffee was thick and smooth, slightly sweet, and although Natalie was still not certain of why she was here, she felt she ought to express appreciation. 'It's good,' she said, and Bilen offered her the bowl of popcorn and biscuits and after she had taken her share, they all ate and although little was said the silence was not fraught or uncomfortable.

The boy finished his biscuit and his popcorn before Natalie and Bilen had drunk their coffee. He held his napkin over his plate and gently shook the crumbs from it. Then he laid it in front of him and turned it over on itself, carefully matching the corners, aligning the edges. When there were no bulges and the fabric lay flat and smooth, he made another fold, and then he took his mother's napkin and repeated the process, placing it neatly beside the other. After this, he reached for Natalie's.

'You can fold hers when she is finished her coffee,' Bilen said.

Natalie frowned, turned towards the window. She pictured the rock in Bilen's hand and how she had risen from her crouching position; the hand without the rock had remained pressed against her left thigh and Natalie guessed at what this must have taken – to rise, and to hide the effort of rising.

'He is always looking at that pool,' Bilen said. 'He thinks you can give him permission to go in. He believes it will be safe if he can see the bottom.'

'Oh,' Natalie murmured. She placed her empty cup down. 'I understand.' She stood and lifted the tray, needing to offer something. 'Shall I put this in the kitchen?' she said.

But Bilen took it from her. 'No,' she said. 'I will do it.' She lowered her voice. 'The fence was broken,' she said, 'but I have driven the nails in with a stone. I have secured the posts.' Very quietly, she added, 'You will no longer be able to pass through in the way you did. I hope you will not mind.'

Bilen turned then and carried the tray to the kitchen, leaning slightly forward, and Natalie recalled how she had placed the rock on the ground and then moved across the yard to her door. She'd walked as if supporting the weight of accumulated experience but at the same time she had appeared taller than she was and somehow lighter.

The boy placed the folded napkins in a line on the shelf. Then he returned to the seat near the window. Standing behind him, Natalie saw that the deckchair was empty now, the man had retreated indoors. The sun had moved so that its angle made bright diamonds on the surface of the water at the shallow end. The vines would grow over the arbour in a year or two, obscuring the outlook, but for now they merely strained the light, making shadows like gauze.

It's Me

K Patrick

SHE CONNECTED BEST WITH her body in winter. It was not quite here, but soon, the leaves already fallen and pounded by shoes. Life more night than day, she liked her torso wrapped, candlelight, birds that withheld, car tyres blurting through puddles. She'd picked up a copy of *In Cold Blood* and managed to read it studiously. Felt, suddenly, that she understood the world in the right technicolour. The book made her feel aware of herself, her own breathing, like a genius, the words swept along in her blood's tidal movements. And if she was a genius, this was the season for it. Mysterious in an ex-boyfriend's bomber jacket. His thermals, too, she liked the bunching of the crotch against her pelvic bone. She'd also wanted to steal his scarf, which had a smell worth possessing, not out of love but a sense of transference, as if his masculinity was an altar easily prepared.

At work she scrubbed a counter and played

over this missed opportunity. He'd been nice enough that he might just have given her the scarf had she asked. She could have framed it as a request for a *momento*. That would have delighted him. To think of her thinking of him, face pressed into the wool, his fantasies had always been exactly that dull.

It was the beautiful hour before opening. A folded darkness through the cafe's display windows, she loved to slip between it, turned on only one light in the backroom. Worked happily in the shadows. She took down the chairs, refilled sugar, salt and pepper. It was difficult to see, grains tipped to the floor, she swept them up again. A few people walked past. Commuters. Burrowed into their heavy coats. To them she would appear only in flashes. Maybe they wondered about her.

She checked the time. The first interruption would be the delivery van, bringing imitation French pastries, cakes, breads. The cafe was a franchise, one of plenty in these richer, smaller towns. People wanted things they could only poorly pronounce. Ranked themselves by a mindless sophistication. If she hurried, and if the driver was on time, there might be a spare five minutes she could use for her book. Otherwise she'd have to wait until her lunch break. She found, if she left it too long between pages, that her genius deteriorated. An apparent failure of memory: it could not maintain enough content to bring forward into her life. Left her at risk of a mortifying sameness.

Fingers warmed in her armpits. The heating took at least an hour to make a difference. Double-checked the long, stainless steel coffee machine. Blasted steam out of the tubes that frothed the milk. The needle on the pressure gauge flickered and then steadied.

Heard his horn. He was on time. She took latex gloves from a box, followed the freakish hygiene guide given to all employees. With the driver she'd worked out an attitude. Spread her legs slightly, folded her arms across her chest, pulled on her chin as they talked, the latex left behind a residue. He was very strong and she wanted to seem the same, he carried the plastic trays of baguettes, chocolate tortes, croissants, able to talk all the while. His wingspan twice as big as hers. It drove her crazy. The handsome vein in his neck, eugh, she found and pinched her own. Before her morning showers she'd begun a routine of press-ups, an attempt to bring more of herself to the surface. Noticed only the strengthening of her wrists, no thickening, her muscles otherwise unchanged. A success so mild she'd most likely invented it. So she carried the trays with pretend gusto, two, three at a time. Looked down so he would not see the effort across her face.

They finished stacking. That's it today. He dusted flour from his hands. Thanks. She positioned her body opposite his, liked the small talk. You getting on OK? Yep, ready for spring but it feels miles away. I don't mind this time of year. He raised his eyebrows. Really? Then yawned like a lion, it was large and alarming, forced her to think of his sleeping habits, how he left his sheets, what time he had to wake up for work. Afterwards he swallowed chunkily. Wrapped his tongue around his front teeth. You must be the only one. Maybe, probably. He looked up at the sky, no stars, hoping it would prove his point. She followed the tilt of his head. Faint moonlight moved quick as steam, clouds fast. More rain later. Yeh most likely. Handed her the invoice and opened up the van door. Saluted as he reversed out onto the quiet road.

She made the sandwiches at speed. Baguettes split and buttered. Nothing French about the vats of margarine. She always tried, at first, to continue working in the dark, until she inevitably cut herself, running the bread knife across her fingernail. Brie and cranberry. Wet ham and cheese. From plastic bags she pulled handfuls of rocket like cut hair. Keys turned in the front door and she knew it would be the manager, the atmosphere soon to be spoiled. Crack of the

IT'S ME

switches, the brutal overhead lights of the cafe came on. Felt the sound of her sigh as the manager appeared in the doorway. Honestly, why do you insist on standing around in the dark? It's calming. Please, are you serious, it's work, it isn't supposed to be calming.

The manager was good-looking and tired. Hair in a tight bun. She would let it down once a day, now, after removing her coat, readjusting, hair-tie between her teeth as she swept it up again, pulling the bun even tighter. The office took up a tiny section of the backroom, next to the giant fridge, opposite the sink and food prep area. It had a lonely computer, ancient, an even lonelier peg for the keys. Only a metre wide, the manager was forced to shuffle inelegantly into her spinning chair, which, if actually spun, would slam her elbows into the wall, her knees into the desk. Once sitting she could hold herself precisely still, cross her legs, let one foot almost slip from her shoe.

She carried the finer cakes to the fridge and set them on stands. Wiped strawberry cream from her sleeve. Arranged beige pastries on a shelf above. They would open shortly. No time to return to her book. The sun arrived low and would stay that way, startling around certain town bends and buildings, reaching the cafe in slow-moving swatches of orange. She turned around the open sign and tightened her blue apron. The book stuck in a grisly locker, the radiators snapping with too much heat, her winter erased. If she was unlucky, her ex-boyfriend would come in, wearing his scarf, and sullenly order an espresso. A drink he didn't like but insisted upon.

The manager wore ugly heels designed for a much older person, wanted comfort while at work, her arches supported. She clacked between the tables. Ready? Ready. The door unlocked. A few women hovered on the pavement. Still fledgling despite their later years, eyelids patted sky blue, hair daring with streaks of pink. They linked arms, would joke melancholically about age. Tried not to rush in once they realised they were allowed. Gazed into the fridges and began calorie counting, fussing over the right table though there were only a few to choose from. Each ordered a cappuccino. She watched them gently drag off the powdered chocolate and lick the spoon. Tore croissants into pieces. Asked for extra jam. Their little routine. The manager returned to the office, would scroll through more lists, make her orders, send emails to who knows. She wished she might be able to read in the lulls, like now, steal a few sentences, rise above her setting. Wanted to go back over the introduction. It was declared Truman Capote was nicknamed Bulldog at school. Another thing she wanted for herself, a new piece of her past designed and introduced. To be called Bulldog, to have spent her adolescence enjoying the fact of an angular, tense face, a pouted bottom lip. Named not only for the animal but after a journalist, the way he had a notebook and pen always in hand, observing, even at eleven.

Another round please! More cappuccinos. A woman peered into the fridge, grey pushed at her pink roots. Maybe something else to eat and why not! Announced to herself, to anybody listening. She smiled, agreed, recommended the small fruit tartlets, only a mouthful after all! Made sure to echo the woman's grammar. That was how to get tips. The jar sat pathetic by the till. An employee before her had grown the word with flowers, turned the dot above the i into a smiley face. She fantasised, and weren't fantasies part of her new genius, about the manager accidentally calling her Bulldog in front of the customers, then blushing, correcting herself. The women took the tartlets, her friends gathered around the plate, oh you shouldn't have, oh but I did.

She was changing, and unlike adolescence she was changing because she wanted to, but it seemed so insincere, to only be able to affect the immediate. She might never be a Bulldog. She had never been a Bulldog. She wiped up dribbled milk.

More customers arrived, anxious about space, would they all fit. A group of six, and one more, they chimed, one more will join us. She helped them drag tables together. Young, colleagues, in clean shirts. The weather had turned. They shook umbrellas, a few worked water out of their hair, shivered so they'd be noticed as cold.

Sorry about all that. One broke away and came to the till. Simple make-up, a big mouth, her lips glossed. A thick bob forced behind her ears. She'd made attempts to contain herself. The effort showed. She tugged at her collar. Reached around to itch her back. No problem. Really, we're literally about to order a million coffees, so it will be a problem soon. Honestly, it's fine. At the centre of the woman's thumb was a bright bruise, burnt green, her nails bitten short. In her word, *million*, the kind emphasis of it, a familiarity clawed at her. Must be a tick from childhood, with *million* this woman had betrayed herself, showed up her ill-fitting suit. Short and broad, seams squeezed, shoulders transported from elsewhere. And there was the sense of a bear about her, not that she'd ever seen a bear, not in real life, but it seemed her humanness could be quickly cast aside.

I guess I'll get things going. She grinned. Just, I don't know, what do people usually get? Cappuccinos are all the rage. I guess I better go with that. She realised then that she did know her, the childhood *million*, the tepid *I guess*, that they had gone to school together, only in the same class for a year, but long enough to become friends. It was a jolt. Seeing her now, understanding the bear body, how it had been ripped from its context, that they had once shared a single worn plastic chair, tried to write their names while holding the same pen. They'd both changed enough that they could not easily find one another here, in this cafe. And how long had it been? Nine years? From fourteen until now? Found she could not announce her recognition. Instead she agreed to the cappuccino and turned her back to make it, grabbing the large white cup, setting down a saucer, feeling a pulse in her lower spine, her tailbone, some murky and resonate piece of skeleton. Hoped that when she moved back to the counter she would be gone, lost to her colleagues, all matching from a distance.

Yes, she was back in a chair and did not look up. Chatted to the woman next to her. Both with their palms stuck to their faces, nodding in turn. Others now queued, asking for their cappuccinos, double shot, single shot, extra chocolate, don't be shy with the chocolate.

Somebody clapped their hands. Announced RIGHT, FOOD and permitted the others to make a choice. Waved a silver credit card and winked. Breakfast is on the company! OK. Shall I give this to you now? She kept waving, her voice loud and unoriginal. Sure. This was hardly a place to be known. The apron, the stains on her sleeve, the silver credit card.

Fine hair, braces. She handed out danishes and palmiers. Fine hair but lots of it, braces like snagged starlight, but she'd been ashamed of them, sealed her lips, even when smiling. What was her name? Elle. Elle. It seemed easier to say this, to call it loudly from where she'd paused, to the right of the coffee machine, pretending to recycle pints of finished milk so she could bend towards the ground and catch her breath. Checked the time. Stalled at 9am. Minutes, seconds, turned solid as sculptures. Hours until an escape, back to her book and her bad men. Capote's bad men. The dark pleasure of his searching, love bloomed like mould, he made you wait for the murders. She was motivated, infuriated, her opinions soared. There Elle sat. She did most of the listening, another colleague told a long story, most likely to do with their office, a petty scandal. Finally, the punchline. When Elle laughed she rolled back her lips. A bear with perfect teeth. She missed, with a pang, the braces, their slicing shame.

The manager opened the connecting door a crack. Motioned for a coffee. She liked a latte three times a day. It had to be piping hot otherwise she'd request, with great sadness, to have it remade.

IT'S ME

In the first days of the job she'd tried to reheat it in the convection oven. The tall glass cracked, the milk burned to the machine in brown bubbles. A furious smell. Like torched fur.

More customers. Disappointed at the lack of space. The latte would have to wait, it made her happy, to keep the manager waiting. A man and woman squeezed themselves onto the remaining seats. Huffed, put out by the large group. Wanted tea, wondered why there were no scones, took ham and cheese baguettes. The husband, she noticed the wedding rings, was bossy but tried to hold it back. His expression puckered. Knew where he wanted to sit but insisted his wife decide. She dithered. His trousers hoiked as he lowered himself into a chair. Revealed slumped socks, skinny chapped ankles.

She slowly swept the floor. Would delay the latte as long as possible. Rain streaked the windows. Her ex-boyfriend's scarf had been red, as if from a child's cartoon for boys, wool but softened slightly, like felt. His scent, embedded in the fabric, had been very good. Memorable, high seas and shrubbery, he had money, his cologne international and hard to find. She had tried for a while, in lieu of the scarf, to track it down. Failed. When they fucked he'd move her face, believing in eye contact, that he could shift her deeper waters. Did not understand how easily he gave away his deeper waters, that he believed in himself and meant it, that he was the protagonist in his own, agonising truth. Men knew nothing about masculinity. It thrilled her.

The manager's face appeared again, she raised an eyebrow, tapped her wrist where there was no watch. One sec. She finished her pointless sweeping, edged the brush into pristine corners. The manager did not like games. Stepped into the cafe. Hissed, it's clean enough, my latte, if you wouldn't mind, if I'm not disturbing you. Her solid cheekbones, her height, turned the customers' heads, she rolled her eyes for their benefit, you just can't find the staff these days! The table of colleagues nodded emphatically. All except Elle who looked off to one side. Focused on a corner of the room. It embarrassed her, it embarrassed them both. The manager leaned next to the coffee machine. Watched closely as she warmed the milk gently, packed in the coffee. Took a sip. Not bad. Lifted it to the room, triumphant, as she left.

Elle got up as the door closed. Ran her eyes along the food, chose nothing. Arrived at the till. She seems like fun. Very. Always like that? Yeh. She spoke in an exacting whisper. Shoulders bulged beneath her polyester. I know the feeling. With her head made a tiny gesture at the table behind, isolating, she assumed, her own boss, most likely the woman with the silver credit card. For a second, maybe two, they were daring in their eye contact. There was no hint of a before, their before, only a consideration of the immediate other, Elle chewing her lip, thoughtful about something else. She tensed her forearms, gripped the cracked plastic countertop. You at least spit in it? Oh, there's never enough time for revenge. Elle snapped her tongue against the roof of her mouth. Surprised to find another piece of her past self that had survived, this signal of appreciation, sounding across nine entire years. No, I suppose there isn't. Tragic, really. Yeh.

They had become friends unexpectedly. Elle had been gentle. Unlike her. Suspected, on reflection, that she might have been unnecessarily cruel at school, never outright a bully, but liked to roam about with the boys, hint at being a slut, and back then, without actual sex, it meant putting people down. They'd bonded over English. Accidental, not dissimilar to now, shared a look across a room occupied with other business, not their business, and in that one look they'd formed a privacy. Held the silence of monks. Solemn, intense. Hadn't it been during a lesson on First World War poets? Even at fourteen, with a fourteen year old's scale of disaster, they'd felt it together, the bitterness, the hot blood, bodies bent and blown by chaos. Siegfried Sassoon, Wilfred Owen, hags, sludge and scraggy knees. Boys dead, what was the line, and God would not give them antlers through their curls, nor talons for their feet. She hadn't forgotten, not really. Until now there had been no reason to remember. Could be her genius had started elsewhere. Sooner. A technicolour found and then abandoned.

Antlers through curls, talons at their feet, yes, or at least something similar. Elle returned to sitting. Watchful, now, though, she could sense it. Eyes down on the table until she turned around to make another coffee, and then she could feel her, tunnelling between the tendons of her neck.

It was not recognition, or even if it was, they did not dare say each other's names, no, she wanted their names to wait and keep on waiting. She collected plates, started with the couple, then down towards the larger group. Moved behind Elle's back, reached over her shoulder to take her empty coffee cup. Actually I'm not quite finished. She put her hand around her wrist, loosely, released her fingers slowly, absentmindedly. Stayed in the conversation that happened around her. She watched Elle's bruised thumb touch her index finger, then move a millimetre north to round her mound of Venus. The table gleefully discussed a colleague's birthday while she was in the bathroom. Wanted a slice of cake they could sink a candle into. They waited for her suggestion. How about the ganache? Like dark chocolate? Yeh. Considered it amongst themselves. Fabulous! Perfect! The candle, pink and already used, was handed to her, she was charged with lighting it, with beginning the song. Elle returned her gaze to the tabletop. The woman with the unoriginal voice added AND PUT IT ALL ON THE CARD.

Her genius had led her here. She lay the candle beside the credit card. Lunch a *million* miles away. On her haunches, lowered to the cabinet, she cut a piece of the cake. Then cut another, for herself, to be eaten later. She would put it on the card. Did not wear her latex gloves. Dragged her pinky through the cake's edge, icing piled up, and right there she sucked it clean. Lifted her eyes and saw Elle was back to watching her, this time unafraid, she wanted to be caught. Kept her face placid, as if she had seen nothing. She straightened and watched her in return, felt the thud of those solid seconds, twisted pieces of brass knocked her skull, her shoulders. A mouthful of them.

For a while she'd had no memories at all, it took determination, to wipe the slate clean and start again, to feel a self finally rise out of the blankness that had been her life. When her ex-boyfriend came, still inside her, he'd sob softly, as if someone at the foot of the bed, just out of her sight, held up an autocue that read (NOW SOB SOFTLY). She'd felt then, if she'd only clamped her thighs hard enough, that she could remove his dick and keep it for her own. Did all geniuses think like this? The charged altitude of her thoughts. She knew that fantasies lasted, that reality forced them into confession, the nasty sort of eternal, etched into stone. The only place fantasy left a trace was the body. Allowed to change, to breathe, to animal.

Neither gave in. She stood still. Let the watching churn through her chest like a water mill. Thought of antlers sprouted through her curls, talons pushing at the heels of her trainers, the murders that would happen at the end. Could taste the chocolate in her mouth. It was the most expensive thing you could order, the chocolate used was virtually a delicacy, gold leaf strayed across the dark surface. The woman emerged from the bathroom. Wiped her hands on her navy blue skirt. The table looked at her urgently, washing out Elle's stare. Now was the time. She lit the candle. Started the opening notes to Happy Birthday as she walked past the till. Elle, along with the others, looked at the woman, whose hands had sprung to her cheeks, turning left and right, saying you shouldn't have, really, my goodness, you shouldn't have, the catchphrase that haunted the cafe. Surrounded by her colleagues who cheered and clapped.

They had kissed only once. Chaste, alone in the classroom, Elle's braces slashed her bottom lip.

The same monastic silence. Love, then, only a mild creature. What do you think, she'd asked afterwards. I guess I would do it again. On the blackboard in front, the names of their poets, their ages, their brief themes. Me too I think. What they could not have known is that they had been seen, through the square glass set above the door, by the teacher. Everything dealt with in a caring and terrified way. Not like that, they'd insisted through a meeting, it's not like that, not when you're older, when you're old enough you'll realise. She had stayed at the school and Elle had left, that Christmas, in January she was nowhere to be seen. Remembered relief and lust. Did not try to find her and felt no regret. Waited, instead, for the kind of future that had been promised.

The table tucked a million tiny forks into the cake. Closed their eyes in a shared ecstasy. It was finished quickly, chairs tired across the floor, they had to get back to work, what a shame. The woman studied her bill but did not notice the extra slice. Surprised to find she tipped generously, a note tucked into the jar. Thank you. No, thank YOU.

Elle took her time. Slipped off her jacket with the missing button, dusted the front, put it back on again. Pulled a pen from an inside pocket and scribbled something down on a napkin. The last to leave, others chatted on the pavement. Did not make her eye contact until the final second, looking up from her shoes only inches from the till. Really, thanks for putting up with us. No problem. She grinned again, and how new, how unnerving it was, to see her mouth, those perfect rows of teeth, no glimmering metal. It was nice meeting you. Same. Yeh? She raised an eyebrow. Participated in an unknown code, it took root in her stomach. Yeh. Good, that's good. She glanced out the window at her colleagues, who danced a little in the wind's chill, but were otherwise absorbed in duller gossip, husbands, sick days, missing items from the office fridge.

Elle cracked her knuckles. This is maybe cheesy, and I don't usually do this, but if you fancied getting a drink sometime, I know a place. She twisted the napkin in her hand. I don't know, you seem cool, I wasn't totally sure, you know, but feels like there's something there?

Still Elle had not recognised her. Wondered if she should she say it now? Announce herself, announce them both, commit each other to stone? Elle handed over the napkin. She reached out and took it from her. Found a number written in blue, a looped sentence that read, *It's me, E!* I'd like that. Yeh? Nice one. Elle was pleased. Unafraid to show it. Bumped her fists, bigger and lovelier, against the countertop. Elle had not only grown into herself but exceeded it, a body that shifted the atmosphere. Lifted her hands, opened one and laid it over the other. Well that's great news, give me a call, yeh? I will. Waved as she went outside, just before the door closed, then again through the glass as the group departed.

She waved back. Watched her gait, her big back, unhurried despite the rain, disappear down the street. Could taste the brass of her mouth. In her mind, pressed the napkin between the pages of her book. Planned the spot. In between the introduction's final words and the first chapter. Heard the manager swear through the door, the disobedient computer, in preparation she pulled down a glass for her second latte.

About the Authors

Nick Mulgrew grew up in South Africa and New Zealand. He is the founder and publisher of the poetry press uHlanga, and is the author of two collections of poetry, two volumes of short stories and two novels. Previously shortlisted for The White Review Prize, Nick also received the Nadine Gordimer Award for his collection, *The First Law of Sadness*. He lives in Edinburgh.

K Patrick is a writer based in Glasgow. Their poetry has appeared in *Poetry Review*, *Granta* and *Five Dials*, and was shortlisted for *The White Review* Poet's Prize in 2021, the same year that K was also shortlisted for *The White Review*'s Short Story Prize. In 2020 they were runner-up in the Ivan Juritz Prize and the Laura Kinsella Fellowship. Their debut novel, *Mrs S*, published by Fourth Estate (UK) and Europa (US) was selected as an *Observer* Best Debut of the Year, and K was named a *Granta* Best of Young British Novelists for 2023.

Their debut poetry collection, *Three Births*, will be published by Granta Poetry in 2024.

Cherise Saywell is a novelist and short story writer. She was born and brought up in Australia and studied English and Cultural Studies at Queensland University. She travelled to the UK in 1996 and has lived in Scotland ever since. She has published two novels, *Desert Fish* (2011) and *Twitcher* (2013) (both Vintage, Australia). Cherise's short stories have won the Pindrop Short Story Award (2016), the Mslexia Short Story Prize (2015) and the V.S. Pritchett prize (2003) as well as being shortlisted for several prizes, including the Bristol Prize (2019) and the Asham Award (2009). Her work has appeared in *Mslexia*, *The London Magazine*, *New Writing Scotland*, and several anthologies, most recently *A Short Affair* (Scribner). Her story 'Pieces of Mars Have Fallen to Earth' was selected for BBC Radio 4's *Opening Lines* programme in 2015. Cherise has been a Royal Literary Fund (RLF) Fellow at Stirling University and Strathclyde University. She now works on the RLF's Bridge project in secondary schools, and as an RLF Consultant in universities. She lives in Edinburgh with her family.

Kamila Shamsie is the author of eight novels, which have been translated into over 30 languages.

ABOUT THE AUTHORS

Home Fire (2018) won the Women's Prize for Fiction, was longlisted for the Man Booker Prize, and shortlisted for the Costa Prize. A Vice-President and Fellow of the Royal Society of Literature and Professor of Creative Writing at the University of Manchester, she was one of Granta's 'Best of Young British Novelists' in 2013. She grew up in Karachi, and now lives in London. Her most recent novel is *Best of Friends* (2022), which was shortlisted for the Indie Book Awards.

Naomi Wood is the bestselling author of three novels and an upcoming collection of stories. Naomi's stories have been published in the *Washington Square Review*, *Joyland*, *S Magazine* and *Stylist*. They have been also shortlisted for the Desperate Literature Prize, the Manchester Fiction Prize, the London Magazine Prize and longlisted for the Galley Beggar Press Prize. Her novels include *The Godless Boys*, *Mrs Hemingway* and *The Hiding Game*. Her first story collection, *This is Why We Can't Have Nice Things*, will come out with Orion in 2024. She lives in Norwich with her family, and teaches Creative Writing at UEA.

About the BBC National Short Story Award with Cambridge University

THE BBC NATIONAL SHORT STORY AWARD is one of the most prestigious and the best rewarded prizes for a single short story and celebrates the best in home-grown short fiction. The ambition of the award, which is now in its eighteenth year, is to expand opportunities for British writers, readers and publishers of the short story, and to honour the UK's finest exponents of the form. The award is a highly regarded feature within the literary landscape with a justified reputation for genuinely changing writers' careers.

James Lasdun secured the inaugural award in 2006 for 'An Anxious Man'; in the years that have followed winners and shortlistees have ranged from the very established – Hilary Mantel, Zadie Smith and Deborah Levy to name but three – to exciting newcomers, from Kiare Ladner to Ingrid Persaud to Anna Bailey. One of the most pleasing outcomes of the Award has been the number of short story collections – over twenty to date – that publishers have invested in following a shortlisting or win: from K. J. Orr to D. W. Wilson, M. J. Hyland to Sara Maitland. The Award makes a tangible difference to many. As a result of her win in 2018, Ingrid Persaud was courted by multiple agents, signed with Rogers Coleridge & White literary agency, sold her debut novel *Love After Love* to Faber & Faber in a seven-way auction and went on to win the Costa First Novel Award 2020. Jo Lloyd, winner in 2019 for 'The Invisible', a long time short story writer, also found an agent and published her first collection of short stories. Not all winners are new names – some of the best authors writing and focusing on the tricky craft of the short story have also taken the prize: In 2020, Sarah Hall won the Award for the second time with 'The Grotesques' – the first two-time winner in the Award's history, followed by Lucy Caldwell in 2021, for 'All the People Were Mean and Bad'. In 2022, Saba Sams won the Award for 'Blue 4eva', celebrated by the judges for its 'utter truthfulness' and 'authentic portrayal of the dynamics of familial relations'. Other alumni include Lionel Shriver, Jon McGregor, Rose Tremain and William Trevor.

The winning author receives £15,000, and the four shortlisted writers £600 each. All five shortlisted stories are broadcast on BBC Radio 4 and all the authors are interviewed on Radio 4's flagship Arts programme, Front Row.

In 2015, to mark the National Short Story Award's tenth anniversary, the BBC Young Writers' Award was launched. Aiming to inspire the next generation of short story writers, to raise the profile of the form with a younger audience, and to provide an outlet for their creative talents, the teenage writers shortlisted for the award have their stories recorded by professional actors for the YWA podcast, and are interviewed on BBC Radio One and in the media. Several young writers, including Brennig Davies, Reyah Martin and Lottie Mills are all now publishing – Lottie's first collection is out next year.

To inspire the next generation of short story readers, teenagers around the UK are also involved in the BBC National Short Story Award via the BBC Student Critics' programme, which gives selected 16 to 18-year-olds the opportunity to read, listen to, discuss and critique the five shortlisted stories. The students are supported with discussion guides, teaching resources and interactions with writers and judges, for an enriching experience that brings literature to life, developed in collaboration with the University of Cambridge.

2018 marked the start of an exciting

partnership between the BBC and the University of Cambridge. The University of Cambridge supports both awards and the Student Critics' programme, and hosts a number of short story events for young writers. An experience day for the YWA shortlistees, hosted by one of the university colleges, includes a taster of university life, dedicated writing seminars and a curated exhibition from the University Library's archive or the Fitzwilliam Museum, to further inspire and intrigue the young writers.

Each year we know that both the Awards and the Student Critics programme discover and celebrate new voices and exciting fiction. 2023 is no exception.

For more information on the awards, please visit www.bbc.co.uk/nssa and www.bbc.co.uk/ywa. You can also keep up-to-date on Twitter via #BBCNSSA, #BBCYWA and #shortstories

Award Partners

BBC Radio 4 is the world's biggest single commissioner of short stories, attracting audiences of over a million listeners. Contemporary stories are broadcast every week, the majority of which are specially commissioned throughout the year.
www.bbc.co.uk/radio4

BBC Radio 1 is the UK's No.1 youth station, targeting 15 to 29 year-olds with a distinctive mix of new music and programmes focusing on issues affecting young people. The station is the soundtrack to young people's lives in the UK and has been for over 50 years.
www.bbc.co.uk/radio1

The University of Cambridge is one of the world's top ten leading universities, with a rich history of radical thinking dating back to 1209. Its mission is to contribute to society through the pursuit of education, learning and research at the highest international levels of excellence. The University comprises 31 autonomous Colleges and 150 departments, faculties and institutions. Its 24,450 student body includes more than 9,000 international students from 147 countries. In 2022, 72.9% of its new undergraduate students were from state schools and 21.2% from economically disadvantaged areas. Cambridge research spans almost every discipline, from science, technology, engineering and medicine through to the arts, humanities and social sciences, with multi-disciplinary teams working to address major global challenges. Its researchers provide academic leadership, develop strategic partnerships and collaborate with colleagues worldwide. The University sits at the heart of the 'Cambridge cluster', in which more than 5,300 knowledge-intensive firms employ more than 67,000 people and generate £18 billion in turnover. Cambridge has the highest number of patent applications per 100,000 residents in the UK. The BBC National Short Story Award is being supported by the School of Arts and Humanities, Faculties of English and Education, University Library, Fitzwilliam Museum and the new University of Cambridge Centre for Creative Writing which is part of the University of Cambridge's Institute of Continuing Education based at Madingley Hall,

AWARD PARTNERS

which provides a range of courses to members of the public, including English Literature and Creative Writing.
www.ice.cam.ac.uk/bbcshortstory

Previous Winners

2022: 'Blue4Eva' by Saba Sams

2021: 'All the People Were Mean and Bad' by Lucy Caldwell

2020: 'The Grotesques' by Sarah Hall

2019: 'The Invisible' by Jo Lloyd

2018: 'The Sweet Sop' by Ingrid Persaud

2017: 'The Edge of the Shoal' by Cynan Jones

2016: 'Disappearances' by KJ Orr
Runner-up: 'Morning, Noon & Night' by Claire-Louise Bennett

2015: 'Briar' by Jonathan Buckley
Runner-up: 'Bunny' by Mark Haddon

2014: 'Kilifi Creek' by Lionel Shriver
Runner-up: 'Miss Adele Amidst the Corsets' by Zadie Smith

2013: 'Mrs Fox' by Sarah Hall
Runner-up: 'Notes from the House Spirits' by Lucy Wood

PREVIOUS WINNERS

2012: 'East of the West' by Miroslav Penkov
Runner-up: 'Sanctuary' by Henrietta Rose-Innes

2011: 'The Dead Roads' by D W Wilson
Runner-up: 'Wires' by Jon McGregor

2010: 'Tea at the Midland' by David Constantine
Runner-up: 'If It Keeps On Raining'
by Jon McGregor

2009: 'The Not-Dead & the Saved' by Kate Clanchy
Runner-up: 'Moss Witch' by Sara Maitland

2008: 'The Numbers' by Clare Wigfall
Runner-up: 'The People on Privilege Hill'
by Jane Gardam

2007: 'The Orphan and the Mob' by Julian Gough
Runner-up: 'Slog's Dad' by David Almond

2006: 'An Anxious Man' by James Lasdun
Runner-up: 'The Safehouse' by Michel Faber